Praise for the Novels
of Tate Hallaway

"[Hallaway's] concise writing style, vivid descriptions, and innovative plot all blend together to provide the reader with a great new look into the love life of witches, vampires, and the undead."
—Armchair Interviews

"What's not to adore?. . . Tate Hallaway has a wonderful gift, Garnet is a gem of a heroine, and *Tall, Dark & Dead* is enthralling from the first page."
—MaryJanice Davidson, *New York Times* bestselling author of *Undead and Unworthy*

"Tate Hallaway kept me on the edge of my seat . . . a thoroughly enjoyable read!"
—Julie Kenner, *USA Today* bestselling author of *Demon Ex Machina*

"Curl up on the couch and settle in—*Tall, Dark & Dead* is a great way to pass an evening."
—Lynsay Sands, *New York Times* bestselling author of *Tall, Dark & Hungry*

"Will appeal to readers of Charlaine Harris's Sookie Stackhouse series."
—*Booklist*

"This paranormal romance overflows with danger, excitement, and mayhem; however, whenever things become too stressful, a healthy dose of irony or comedy shows up to ease the way. Tate Hallaway has an amazing talent for storytelling." —Huntress Book Reviews

"Funny and captivating . . . in the style of the Sookie Stackhouse series [with] an intrepid and expressive heroine. . . . Look out, fans of the paranormal, there's a new supernatural heroine in town. . . . Tate Hallaway is an author to watch!" —Romance Reviews Today

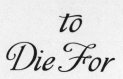

A VAMPIRE PRINCESS NOVEL

 TATE HALLAWAY

NEW AMERICAN LIBRARY

NEW AMERICAN LIBRARY
Published by New American Library, a division of
Penguin Group (USA) Inc., 375 Hudson Street,
New York, New York 10014, USA
Penguin Group (Canada), 90 Eglinton Avenue East, Suite 700, Toronto,
Ontario M4P 2Y3, Canada (a division of Pearson Penguin Canada Inc.)
Penguin Books Ltd., 80 Strand, London WC2R 0RL, England
Penguin Ireland, 25 St. Stephen's Green, Dublin 2,
Ireland (a division of Penguin Books Ltd.)
Penguin Group (Australia), 250 Camberwell Road, Camberwell, Victoria 3124,
Australia (a division of Pearson Australia Group Pty. Ltd.)
Penguin Books India Pvt. Ltd., 11 Community Centre, Panchsheel Park,
New Delhi - 110 017, India
Penguin Group (NZ), 67 Apollo Drive, Rosedale, North Shore 0632,
New Zealand (a division of Pearson New Zealand Ltd.)
Penguin Books (South Africa) (Pty.) Ltd., 24 Sturdee Avenue,
Rosebank, Johannesburg 2196, South Africa

Penguin Books Ltd., Registered Offices:
80 Strand, London WC2R 0RL, England

First published by New American Library,
a division of Penguin Group (USA) Inc.

First Printing, August 2010
10 9 8 7 6 5 4 3 2

REGISTERED TRADEMARK—MARCA REGISTRADA

LIBRARY OF CONGRESS CATALOGING-IN-PUBLICATION DATA:

Hallaway, Tate.
Almost to die for: a vampire princess novel/Tate Hallaway.
    p. cm.
ISBN 978-0-451-23057-7
1. Teenage girls—Fiction. 2. Vampires—Fiction. 3. Witches—Fiction. 4. Chick lit. I. Title.
PS3608.A54825A79 2010
813'.6—dc22   2010010401

Set in Minion
Designed by Ginger Legato

Printed in the United States of America

For Shawn and Mason

Acknowledgments

I'd like to thank my editor, Anne Sowards, for her vision for this series, and my tireless agent, Martha Millard, for making it happen. I
also need to specially thank those who read the book in process, the
Wyrdsmiths—Bill Henry, Doug Hulick, Kelly McCullough, and
Sean M. Murphy, but particularly my friend and mentor Eleanor Ar-
nason, who kept me company in my dark hours, and Naomi Kritzer,
a great and true friend, who read the whole thing and made it so very
much better.

My family gets a mention as well. Shawn Rounds, of course, who
not only supported me with many *there, theres* but also acts as my
first-run copy editor and plot maven extraordinaire. My son, Mason,
who is a great sounding board for the cool vampire and witchy stuff,
and if you ask him, he'll tell you quite seriously: he figured out the
plot.

To the staff at Amore Coffee in St. Paul, who supplied me with
much-needed caffeine and who patiently listened to me whine about
deadlines and the writer's life, I must also give a huge thanks.

And, of course, my parents, Rita and Mort Morehouse, without
whom none of this, quite literally, would be possible.

Almost
to
Die For

Guess what? Today was my sixteenth birthday. Pretty cool, huh? Sure, if by "cool" you mean worst day ever . . . and it was only noon.

I sat in Stassen High School's cafeteria staring at "tuna surprise." Let me tell you: it was a surprise all right. I was surprised it passed the health code. It was gray, for crying out loud. Food should not be gray.

Also, my birthday might be tolerable if I lived somewhere exciting, but no, I'd be turning sixteen in nowheresville: St. Paul, Minnesota.

I pushed the glutinous mush around its little container. At least the potatoes looked edible. My stomach growled, so I poked a forkful into my mouth. I sighed. What I really wanted was my turkey sandwich, or at least someone I could joke around with about the whole stupid situation.

But no. I was sitting alone.

Bea was supposed to be here. Sometime in middle school we

had made a solemn blood vow. We'd always sit together at lunch so neither of us would ever have to look like that sad, lonely loser.

Hello—yes, that'd be me! Loser in corner number one.

On my birthday, no less.

Bea—Beatrice Theodora Braithwaite to her mother—was my kind-of sort-of best friend. She was the only person in school with a more arcane name than I. Get a load of this: Anastasija Ramses Parker. Yeah. You can see why most people just call me Ana.

Anyway, Bea and I, we've known each other since second grade. That's a lot of history. It's hard not to be close to someone you borrowed your first tampon from, giggled your way through puppy-love crushes with, and survived that god-awful middle school sex education with. Though, honestly, I don't always like her. We're pretty different. Bea has diva tendencies, and I lean toward being a bookish shrinking violet. But we've been kind of thrown together by fate because she's the only other True Witch at school.

It's a secret, but real magic exists. True Witches can make shit happen. Not just that New Agey feel-good stuff, but, like, things you'd notice: storms, sickness, dead cattle. You know, all the stuff we used to get burned at the stake for. That's why we don't talk about it.

There were plenty of Wiccans at school and elsewhere, of course. It's all the rage to be a teen witch, but Bea and I could do real magic.

Or at least *Bea* could.

I was *supposed* to be able to. I had the pedigree, but, well, something was off. Maybe it was the same *off* something that made one of my eyes ice blue and the other a deep mahogany brown.

When a chair scraped the linoleum floor, I looked up expectantly. Perhaps Queen Bea had finally deigned to put in an appearance. Well, better late than never.

Instead of Bea, it was Matt Thompson, hockey jock extraordinaire, and two of his cronies, Thing One and Thing Two, who sat down at my table. Between you and me, I had this secret crush on Thompson. He was pretty in that classic square-jaw, he-man way, okay? I appreciated the way his ultrashort, nut-brown hair curled at the tips, and the boy did have a way of fitting into a T-shirt and jeans that was pretty . . . noticeable.

Too bad he was *such* an asshole.

"If it isn't Ana Parker, Witch Girl." He made it sound like some kind of superhero moniker. His buddies chortled.

I retorted with, "What do you want, Thompson? Did you get lost on your way to Caveman 101?" Which was a pretty snappy comeback for me, considering the quivering in my stomach. Guys like Thompson could smell fear, so I tried to hide mine under an air of contempt.

His friends looked at each other with perfect Neanderthal, heavy-eyebrow frowns and shrugged as if they didn't get the joke. Thompson, meanwhile, didn't let it faze him. "How come you're all on your lonesome, anyway? Couldn't *conjure* up some friends?"

Oh, touché, you maestro of wit and repartee.

Thing One and Thing Two, however, found his little pun absolutely hilarious.

"Right. Ha. Ha," I said. My tough-girl facade cracked a bit. These sorts of scenes never broke in favor of the geek. If I wasn't careful, there was going to be a drink in my face or some other embarrassment in my future. Worse, I knew I'd fare much better if Bea were here as backup. Why were they still harassing me, anyway? Usually Thompson and his crew did flyby potshots and left Bea and me alone. Was this his sad, grade school way of flirting?

"Careful, man," said Thing One. "She might put a hex on us."

I wish. The sad thing was that these three boys were perfectly safe from little ol' me. I was a dud in the magic department. But they didn't know that. No one did, not even Bea. That was my own special secret. One I tried to keep from myself. If I wasn't a True Witch, then I was just a plain old loser, wasn't I?

Ironically, I could tell that underneath the huff and gruff, the boys were a teeny bit nervous at calling me out. After all, if Bea were here, they might easily find a colony of spiders in their gym shorts, or locker combinations that no longer worked.

For real.

The only thing I had going for me was that I totally looked the part of a witch. I had long, wicked straight hair complete with a slight widow's peak right in the center of my pale, pasty forehead. Okay, Bea said my complexion was porcelain, but I always felt ghostly white and washed out . . . except for my eyes. I hardly needed mascara for the thick lashes that made my mismatched eyes stand out. It was my biggest weapon against guys such as Thompson and his crew.

So I turned my patented "spooky eye" on them. It was a look I'd perfected over the years. I squinted directly at Thompson with the ice-cold blue eye. I muttered under my breath about hex and flex and sex and T. rex and other rhyming words because, you know, people expect spells to rhyme.

They looked nervous. Thing Two's Adam's apple bobbed. Glances flitted among them. Thompson tried to act as if he was unimpressed, but suddenly he saw someone he knew across the room. "Hey, there's Yvonne. I need to talk to her about the band coming to her house party." As he stood up to flee, Thompson mustered one last bit of nasty. "Too bad you'll never be popular enough to be invited to a house party, freak."

"Boo!" I said.

Thompson jumped and uttered a sound not unlike a squeak. Thing One—or maybe it was Two—actually snickered.

Score one for the freak! I only wished I didn't feel like he might be right about me. Thompson swaggered over to flirt with Yvonne Jackson, whom everyone figured he'd take to homecoming, since she was, after all, the captain of the cheerleading squad. So cliché. I watched them surreptitiously as I attempted to ingest the edible parts of lunch. He leaned in to talk to her, propping himself on the table with his elbows, which made his pecs bulge. She giggled. It was gross, really, but . . .

Here I was, turning sixteen on the sixteenth, and was I having any kind of party? Would there be music and dancing or anything cool? Would I get any presents? No. Tonight, what I had to look forward to was a long, boring drive to a cabin in the far suburbs while Bea and my mom chatted on like the whole thing wouldn't flop.

The cabin was our "covenstead," the place where our group of those capital-letter True Witches practiced magic in secret. Once there, I'd get to fail spectacularly in front of everyone when

I was called on to perform a simple elemental spell as part of my official Initiation, or welcoming into the Inner Circle.

Only there wouldn't be any welcoming.

Because after I fubared the ritual, my mother would cry. I'd be shunned, cast out of the coven, and I'd finish my days at Stassen High School just like this: sitting alone at lunch, while everyone—*every*one, even Bea—thought I was a weirdo freak.

It was going to be *so* awesome.

And I still hadn't even made it halfway through the day yet. Whee.

Two

caught up with Bea right before sixth-period drama class. Even though I'm pretty shy most of the time, I love theater. I've been in every play since I scored the part of the crazy sister in *The Madwoman of Chaillot* in junior high. Of course, I'm usually typecast: one of the three Wyrd Sisters in *Macbeth*, the Wicked Witch of the West in *Wizard of Oz*, Medea in *Medea*, etc. But theater was the one place my odd looks actually played to my advantage.

"Where were you at lunch?" I asked her. We'd stopped outside her locker, which was right next to Mr. Martinez's drama class. She dropped her math book into the pile of detritus cluttering the floor of the tiny space. I wondered whether she'd find it again without sending in a search party. "I had to sit by myself."

"Aw, poor baby," she teased. She patted my cheek patronizingly. "Ooo had to sit all by ooo-self."

Did I mention that I sometimes didn't like Bea all that much?

I shrugged it off. I mean, I knew she didn't mean any harm. She always rallied on the side of sisterhood when it mattered. "Yeah, well, you missed me giving Thompson the evil eye."

"I heard about that, actually." Bea smiled and looped her arm around mine as if I were escorting her ladyship to the ball. We must have looked quite the pair. She had on a black jumper over a pink-and-black-striped, long-sleeved shirt and matching leggings. She wore her hair in girlish pigtails that showed off the pink streaks in her dyed black hair.

For myself, I'll admit that I adhered to the Goth palette. It was black with black and black for me, though in deference to my birthday I'd jazzed up my usual slim jeans, tank top, and long-sleeved button-up with a heavy silver ankh necklace and my fancier boots.

"What was it you heard?" I asked, pausing just outside the door to class.

"That you hexed him. He tripped in chemistry class and spilled some kind of crazy acid all over the table. They had to get out the hazmat suits to clean it up. You go, girl."

I frowned at Bea's exaggeration. I was sure there were no hazmat suits involved. More to the point, I knew I hadn't hexed him. No magic had come out of me. I was certain. I might not have been able to perform a lick of real magic, but I'd always been able to keep my secret because I could feel spells working. I could tell when energy peaked and when anyone around me was using even the smallest amount.

I'd done to Thompson what I'd done my whole life when it came to magic: I faked it.

I let my hand slip from her arm. Bea, meanwhile, was smiling at me like the damned Cheshire cat. "I was wondering when you'd get off your high horse and finally zap somebody," Bea said with a playful poke to my ribs. "The Wiccan Rede is for Wiccans, not True Witches."

It was Bea's favorite thing to say in situations such as this. She didn't really get behind "an it harm none" and all the do-unto-others parts of the Rede. She figured crap like "for the greatest good of all" was for people who couldn't *do* at all. Zap the baddies. That was her motto.

Me, I was less sure. I mean, karma has a way of biting you on the butt when you least expect it.

Luckily I didn't have to respond to Bea because the first bell rang. We hurried into class.

THE ENTIRE CLASS WAS TAKING turns reading lines from Shakespeare's *Twelfth Night* while Mr. Martinez occasionally broke in to explain some ancient terminology or an obtuse (but usually raunchy) joke. I was normally totally into this class, but today my mind wandered.

What Bea suggested about my magic working on Thompson sprouted this crazy hope inside my heart.

What if?

What if turning sixteen had clicked that off-something of mine into an on-something?

Part of me always wondered whether I'd missed some critical lesson that everyone else had gotten. Like, all I needed was some key to turn inside me, and then it would all make sense.

What if it had happened and I could finally really do magic?

I could hardly wait for the bell to ring so I could run home and try out a spell or two. I mean, I had been dreading this Initiation thing since I first realized the depth of my suckage in the witch department. Maybe . . . maybe tonight at the big ritual, things might not be as horrible as I'd always thought they would.

"Ms. Parker? Are you with us?"

I blinked. Mr. Martinez stood in front of my desk, frowning at me. He was a very trim guy, and he always looked sharp in a pressed white shirt and dark slacks and tie. But the sour expression on his face ruined the whole slick look, honestly.

"Uh," I said as I noticed everyone in class staring at me. It must be my turn to read. I looked down at the page, but I had no idea where we were in the play.

"Uh, line?" It was what you said when you forgot what you were supposed to say during a stage rehearsal. As I hoped, I got a few laughs from the veteran actors in class. Mr. Martinez, however, wasn't one of them. In fact, he looked at me like I'd deeply wounded him and that I'd blown my chances for a letter of introduction to Juilliard. Not that I knew what I wanted to do with my life or anything.

"Ana, I expected better of you. Could someone please cue our daydreaming Ms. Parker?"

Hands shot up around the room. Sucking up to Mr. Martinez was a tried-and-true path to audition callbacks. He called on Taylor. Taylor was my best nonwitch friend. She was a gamer, big into theater, and an all-around nerd. In short, my kind of people. Plus, she had the most amusing crush on Mr. Martinez, whom everyone else in the entire class figured to be quite fabulously gay.

She was so getting the lead in the next production.

I, meanwhile, felt more and more like an idiot as the seconds ticked as I scanned the page for the line. Finally I found it and read it with a deep blush spreading across my face. I determined to pay better attention for the rest of the class.

AFTER, THE THREE OF US girlfriends gathered to debrief about the day. Taylor couldn't meet us for lunch because she had it a different period. So, to catch up on everything, we had a tradition of walking one another to our lockers and sharing news, tidbits, and general gossip. Since Bea's was the closest, we always met there.

"Where was your head during class, Ana? Mr. Martinez was right. You're usually an A student," Taylor said.

Taylor was a first-generation Somali and wore her head covered in a sparkly lamé wrap. Her real name was something much more ethnic, but she insisted that everyone call her Taylor. Even though she kept her head covered, she didn't go for the whole long-flowy-dress thing. Instead, she wore jeans, a long-sleeved knit sweater, and cowboy boots. If you couldn't already tell, Taylor was another outsider like us. Even though there were a ton of other Somali girls at school, Taylor was far too strange for them, with her love of graphic novels, video games, and all things geeky.

"I don't know." I shrugged.

Bea, meanwhile, had no comment, as her head was deep in her locker while she rummaged through her things, gathering up what she needed to take home.

"Seriously, you seemed lost in there. Is everything okay?" Taylor asked again.

"I've got a big night tonight," I said. "It's my birthday."

"Oh, are you having a party?" Taylor asked, her voice carrying that you-didn't-invite-me edge.

"A party? I wish," I said. "I have to do a . . ." Hmm, what to say here? We weren't supposed to talk about witchy stuff, but I didn't want to totally evade the question. That was far more suspicious. "A test?"

"You don't sound very sure about it," Taylor noted. She looked more hurt, like she figured I had to be lying about the party and her invitation to it.

"That's because it's more like a graduation," Bea said blithely. "Ana and I are doing a ritual tonight. It's a kind of initiation ceremony. It's all hush-hush, though. Big magic stuff."

I stared at Bea. Well, okay, I guess that was one way to keep the secret. Telling the truth like it was no big deal. But she was playing pretty fast and loose with the rules.

"Oh, it's a religion thing," Taylor said, sounding genuinely relieved. "But you're going to have a party or something this weekend, though, right, Ana?"

"For whom? The three of us?" I asked. I mean, how lame would that be?

Bea shook her head, like I was a world-class fool. "You're sad, you know that? We totally should throw you a birthday party on Saturday. Invite the whole school."

"That'd be epic!" Taylor agreed. "Maybe you could get a hot local band to do a house party. I hear Yvonne is having one. But you know who would be cool to book? That band Nikolai Kirov is in. What's it called?"

"Ingress," Bea said without missing a beat.

"Nikolai from . . ." I stopped myself before saying "coven," but only just barely.

"Yeah, that one," Bea said.

Wow. I had no idea Nikolai was in a band. He'd graduated

from Stassen last year, but I mostly interacted with him in the coven. In fact, he was going to be part of the Initiation tonight.

"He's superhot," Taylor said dreamily.

"Yeah," Bea agreed. She had a crush on him.

He was pretty cute if you liked smoldering, exotic older guys. Which, okay, I did, but even if by some miracle he was interested in me, Bea had it bad for him.

"Yeah, well, it's all a pipe dream. I could never have any kind of party at my house." My mom would never go for it. No one was allowed in the house who wasn't in on the secret of the True Witches, which was almost no one—trust me. I could count on my fingers my friends who'd been invited over. One. Bea.

A party at our house? No way. Mom would have a conniption fit.

"No," Bea said. "Mine. Leave it up to me. I'll organize the whole thing."

Why did I not feel grateful? Instead a deep dread ran through my soul. Bea in charge of my birthday? It was going to turn into something all about her, and nothing like my quiet, sedate self could truly enjoy.

"Uh . . ." I started to try to come up with a reason Bea should rein in her kindness, but then out of the corner of my eye I saw Thompson and his crew coming down the hallway. They looked pissed off and like they were on a mission. Maybe a little witch hunt? I poked Bea in the back. "We should hurry."

Bea looked in the direction I was staring. "Oh yes, I see."

"See what?" Taylor looked confused as she tried to track our gaze. Then she took a sharp breath. "Is Thompson coming over here? To . . . talk to us?"

I pulled Bea by the hand to hurry her along, but it was too

late. Thompson and his cronies had blocked our path. They looked big and menacing. They wore matching letter jackets, like some twisted version of gang colors. The grim looks on their faces made me swallow. Hard.

Next to me, I could feel Bea revving up her magic. I tried to catch her eye to warn her off the idea, but her mouth had compressed into a thin determined line. She gripped my hand tightly and gave me a broad wink. "Zap 'em, sister," she whispered.

Three

At Bea's words, Thompson had the sense to take a step back. But an animalistic snarl covered his fear, and then he poked me hard in the shoulder. It hurt.

"Don't mess with me again, witch," he said. His hands curled into fists. I held my breath. I thought he might actually hit me.

Bea twitched her nose, *Bewitched*-style. I felt a strong zing in the air, like electricity.

"Don't do it," I pleaded, despite my fear. If she put any kind of curse on him, it would only end in more reprisals. There were reasons there were rules against this sort of thing in our community.

"Zap," Bea said quietly, and poked Thompson in the shoulder, like he'd done to me, only much more gently.

"What was that?" he demanded. He stared at the spot on his shoulder like he expected to break out in hives.

"Dude," said Thing One, his eyes wide and wildly looking between Bea and me. "You're totally cursed. I'm out of here."

"Me too," agreed Thing Two.

And just like that, his friends melted into the crowded hall-way. Poof! They were gone. Almost like magic.

Well, okay, actually, *exactly* like magic. Bea's spell had made Thompson instantly unpopular. It would wear off in a couple of days, and he might never even really know what happened and why no one would return his calls or texts or whatever.

But Thompson did notice the absence of his wingmen. He tried to look cool as he said, "Yeah, well, I mean it. Don't screw with me again, freaks." I thought he might back his words up with another physical threat—a shove or something—but in-stead, he looked at each of us in turn, very meaningfully. "Any of you."

We watched him leave. My nerves jangled with unspent adrenaline. Taylor swore under her breath—at least I thought so, because it wasn't in English. She scanned our faces. "What was that all about?"

"Thompson thinks I hexed him at lunch," I said. Of course, now Bea had hexed him for real. Not that I could tell Taylor that.

"Yeah, well, that scared the crap out of me," she snipped be-fore stomping off.

"I'm sorry!" I shouted after her, but she just waved her hand like she didn't want to have anything to do with me or Bea ever again. Not that I could blame her. We *were* freaks. And Thomp-son had seemed ready to pound us into pulp. I didn't know if he'd actually have done something, but I'd never felt that close to getting hit before. My knees trembled.

Bea just flipped her pigtails. I could tell, though, by the way she chewed the black lipstick off her lip, she was upset too. "If they'd actually . . . ," she started, but stopped. She couldn't bring herself to say what we were both thinking. We were used to taunts and teases, but this had seemed different. I could feel Bea's energy humming again, ready to blow.

"Power down," I told her. "You've got no target right now."

Bea took a deep breath. I felt the phantom sensation of my ear popping, as Bea released her magic into the floor.

"I'll call Taylor later," I said.

"It's not Taylor I'm worried about."

"Do you really think they'd have done something?"

"People hate witches. They're scared of us. They always have been. Two words, sister: Burning Times."

I was surprised to hear Bea use the term. It'd been totally co-opted by the Wiccan wannabes. But, granted, it was much more powerful an image than "the Inquisition," which, thanks to Monty Python, had become the butt of a joke. The Inquisition, the Burning Times—whatever you chose to call it—was one big reason we weren't supposed to do what Bea just did. No magic zapping on the regular folks. No talking about how it all really works. Secret keeping was the watchword of True Witches.

Yet Bea just blew our cover in her attempt not to be "burned," as it were. She was the one who'd used the real deal on Thompson. Now we were going to have to deal with the consequences of that.

"I'm going to miss my bus," I said.

Look, didn't I tell you I was shy? I know I should have called Bea on her hypocrisy, but, really, at the end of the day, it wasn't going to matter which one of us used real magic and which one faked it. Thompson considered us the same. We were the spooky girls, the witches.

"Come on," Bea said with a weak smile. "I'll give you a ride home. Besides, I've got a present for you in the car."

I KEPT GLANCING OVER MY shoulder, but I never caught sight of Thompson or any of his cronies. We made it to the school parking lot without further incident. Bea drove this rusty Buick that was as long as a bus and belched the foulest-smelling black smoke whenever she started it up.

Still, she had a ride.

I had neither a car nor a license. I'd gotten a learner's permit last year, but my mom's crazy work schedule made it impossible to get enough hours behind the wheel. The temporary license expired. In a snit, I hadn't gotten a new one. What was the use anyway?

I tossed my backpack into the backseat and buckled myself into the bench seat on the passenger side. The strap was huge and beige and made an ancient clicking sound as it locked in. I felt like I was getting a ride from my grandma in this boat. Bea's car even smelled like an old-lady car. And somehow, despite how she kept her locker and her room, the floors were always clean and free of clutter.

Bea was tiny, barely five feet, so the bench seat was pulled up as far as it could go. My knobby knees knocked against the dash.

"Your present is in the glove compartment," Bea said as she went through the motions of getting ready to drive: buckle, adjust rearview, check mirrors, etc. She was like a textbook in careful driving.

I spread my legs awkwardly to open the latch. On top of a

neat stack of maps was a slim, wrapped box. The paper was sparkly purple, and she'd wrapped it with a cloth bow of a soft lavender color. "It's beautiful," I said.

Bea laughed at me. She turned the key, and the engine roared to life with a huge puff of black smog. "That's just the box, silly."

I tore into the package. The box said it came from Bibelot, a high-end shop known for its exquisite jewelry. "Is this really . . . ?"

"Open it!"

I did as I was told. The necklace inside was gorgeous. I pulled it out to get a better look at it. It was shaped almost like a Christian rosary, but where the crucifix would normally hang was a Nile goddess pendant—a slim abstract shape of a woman with large hips, a long, slender, almost snakelike head, and her arms raised into a loop over her head. In place of prayer beads were mother-of-pearl beads interspersed with black onyx, twenty-eight exactly—the cycle of the moon.

Bea hadn't bought this. It was too personal. Besides, I could feel her energy in every bead and dancing along each wire. "You made this, didn't you?"

Even though her eyes stayed focused on successfully navigating the crowded parking lot, they sparkled with pride. "Do you like it?"

"Are you kidding? This is awesome!" I would have hugged her, but I knew how nervous she got when she drove.

"It took me several months. I had a heck of a time learning to twist the silver wire."

Sometimes when I held handcrafted items, I got the impression of the sweat of hard work or frustration with materials or the artisan's sense of his or her own skill level. Not here. This piece sang to me of joy and love. I let the light play on it in my hands. "No, it's beautiful. I can't believe you made it for me."

"Best friends?" she asked.

"Yeah," I said with a smile. Even though I didn't always like Bea, at heart we were sisters. "Forever."

ONCE OUT OF THE PARKING lot, we headed down Lexington Avenue. It was one of St. Paul's busier thoroughfares, but the road was divided by planted islands. September was almost over, and the grass had begun to brown and die off. The trees hinted at the color to come with patches of orange and yellow still mostly hidden among dark green leaves.

"It's going to be beautiful up at the covenstead," Bea remarked.

The coven communally owned property about an hour and a half north of the Cities. Several generations ago, they'd pooled their money and bought a hundred and fifty acres of undeveloped land. All twelve families used it as their "cabin up north." There was a small, marshy lake we'd all learned to swim in, and deep woods for mushroom hunting and wild-blueberry picking.

As long as I could remember, I'd spent summer up there. It was like my second home. My heart ticked nervously in my ear. "Bea, if I don't pass . . ." I couldn't finish the thought out loud. I loved that place. To be banished was heartbreaking.

She spared a glance at me. "You're so negative, you know that? Remember Thompson? You're going to kick ass."

"I hope you're right," I said, wishing I felt more buoyed by her confidence. When I shifted, my hand brushed Bea's gift. The magic of the necklace electrified the tips of my fingers. Did the things I created hold that kind of power?

I shook my head.

Bea happened to look over at that moment and misinterpreted. "Of course I'm right," Bea said, patting my knee.

I felt sort of patronized, so I said, "Your mom didn't pass."

The moment I spoke, I knew it had been a mistake. Bea's lip twitched into an angry sneer before she could conceal her expression. I'd crossed a line. Honestly, I wasn't sure I was supposed to even know. She never talked about her mom's status in the coven. Most of the time we pretended she'd married into the coven, and that Bea's dad was the only witch of the family.

Bea sniffed. "My mom's a special case. She was cursed."

That was the myth, anyway. But no one ever explained by whom or . . . to what end. It was clear you weren't supposed to ask too many questions either. The one time I did, all I got were vague hints of some outside enemy, which were then quickly followed by how we don't talk about *that*, lest we call the evil present. It always seemed like a handy excuse to me.

That wasn't an opinion I discussed with Bea, though. Best friends or not, family secrets were off-limits. I respected that.

After all, I had my share.

My lineage was "broken." Even with the family curse, Bea, at least, had two parents who came from witch families. At her birth, her name had been written in flourishing script in the big Book of Shadows, wherein all the Names were recorded. She could look at the branching tree and see how her blood connected and interwove all the way back to the First Witch.

My name was yet to be written.

There was a space for it, but it was blank. My mother's name was alone too. No paternal branch listed.

It was like I had no father.

At all.

What I found particularly strange about this was that there were other "regular" people who'd married into the Families. I mean, think about it, you kind of had to go out of your group now and again or we'd all be inbred and weirder than we already were. But *they* were all listed. The book was extremely complete.

Sometimes there was a name, after which was written "May Child." That was a witch way of saying "one-night stand." It had to do with an old practice of wild sex on Beltane, May 1. But even the May blessings were all written down. I knew because I'd noticed even some who died before they turned sixteen got to be named.

Not me.

I was a blank waiting to be filled.

Yet, everyone assumed I'd be there eventually. Whenever Elders showed me the book, they would say, "Here is where you'll be, Ana, after the Initiation."

No pressure or anything.

"I'm going to try a spell when I get home," I told Bea. "You know, to see if Thompson was a fluke or what."

"That's a good idea," she said. "You've been so nervous about this. It'll be good to have some confidence. You know, attitude is half of magic."

Another favorite claim of Bea's, but I just rolled my eyes. She looked ready to give me crap for my reaction, but we'd come to my house.

*   *   *

I JUMPED OUT WITH A quick thanks to Bea because Mom's car was parked out front. It was very recognizable: a bright blue MINI Cooper.

It was weird for her to be home this early. She was an adjunct professor of women's studies. This semester she had more than a full load, and taught at a bunch of different colleges and universities in St. Paul and Minneapolis. She had classes almost every day, and a couple at night. There were office hours to keep and syllabuses to prepare. Plus, there was the constant research and she ran a "study group" on women's mysteries and Dianic (read: feminist, women only) Wicca. I didn't see her much, especially during the beginning of the year.

I approached the house cautiously. Our house was a funky old Victorian, heavy on the funky—a painted lady in need of a fresh coat. The wraparound porch sagged, shrouded in ivy and overgrown mulberry trees. A wrought iron fence made the whole thing look formidable. As silly as it was, I often hesitated before crossing into the yard. Our house was protected by wards that were meant to keep strangers out, but they always worked their magic on me a little bit. I often paused, as if wondering if I were invited into my own home.

I shook off the feeling with a deep, steadying breath.

My garden had been a huge success this year. This was the first year I'd really taken over all the gardening, and I was extremely proud of the results. The glory had faded a bit, but there were still large shocks of bright purple coneflowers and painted daisies in pink, lavender, and baby blue. In the shade, my favorite section grew: forget-me-nots, hostas, and Solomon's seal. If

Mom weren't so controlling about having nonwitches to the house, I could have entered in the Summit Avenue Tea and Garden Show.

I always got a lift when people stopped and hung their heads over the fence to point and remark. If I had any magic at all, it was with growing things.

Smiling, I ascended the steps.

Even two steps up the porch, I could smell a cake baking.

Aw.

I let myself into the house. "Hey, Mom, I'm home!"

"Shit!"

There was crashing and bashing as I hung my backpack on the hook by the door. I pulled off my boots and left them in front of the built-in parson's bench by the bay window. More swearing came from the kitchen.

I wondered whether I should go in. I mean, was it better to sit out here and pretend I hadn't spoiled the cake surprise, or to go in and make a joke about how she usually bought from the store, which would make it all okay?

I wanted to be the sort of person who could make everyone laugh and forget all about the awkward, but I never quite knew what to say or had the joke ready. Anyway, while I was considering my options, Mom came out. She shut the door behind her, which she almost never did. She smoothed her sundress and shook out her long, curly blond-gray hair. "You're home early."

"Bea gave me a ride," I explained.

Mom adjusted her glasses, examining me like I was one of her students come to beg out of a bad grade.

"Well," she said, matter-of-factly, "I'm not ready for you. You're just going to have to busy yourself elsewhere."

"Oh," I said. My mom was like this, very coldly pragmatic, but it still always surprised me. And anyway, what did she expect me to do, exactly? Should I go to the coffeehouse? Take a walk? I glanced at the polished wood banister of the open staircase that led up to my room. "Can I hide out in my room?"

Mom considered this for a moment. "Yes," she agreed with a curt nod. "That would do nicely."

I TOOK MY BACKPACK TO my upstairs exile. My room was one of three bedrooms upstairs. My mom got the largest one, just off the top of the stairs. Mine was straight ahead. Mom and I shared the other room for our various crafts. She sewed. I . . . well, dabbled with a lot of stuff. I had mask-making materials, oil and water paints, charcoal sketches, colored-pencil doodles, hot-glue-gun messes, and other art junk I'd collected over the years.

Everyone always figured I'd end up at MCAD, the Minneapolis College of Art and Design. True Witches had an affinity for the arts, or at least that's what I'd always heard among the Inner Circle types. Half the boards of various art institutions were populated by our Elders. Me, I wasn't so sure. Theater called to me, and, secretly, so did biology . . . and math.

Not that I'd ever confess to being a science geek. Not on pain of death.

It was another secret I hid. Well, Mom could see I got good grades in science, and I was clearly in the advanced math classes, but . . . she could understand the theater stuff better. It suited her image of a True Witch.

I tossed my backpack on my bed. Mom had made the quilt.

Each square had an ancient goddess image. There were strange snake women, bird ladies, and flat-perspective lion-headed Egyptian goddesses. Honestly? I found it a bit "political," but the fabric was wonderfully soft and warm, so I kept it.

In the dormer, I'd situated my desk. I got great afternoon sun to do my homework by, though sometimes the glare sucked for my laptop. My mother and I had fashioned crude bookcases from cinder blocks and boards that fit snugly in the awkward space. In them, I had all my favorite books, manga, and graphic novels.

I sat down in the chair, thinking I might tackle some homework before acting surprised when Mom pulled out the cake. The message icon flashed on my phone. Pulling it off the charger, I read it. "Do ur homework." It was Bea's way of reminding me to try out my spell. She'd finished it with, "Zap!"

Spinning in my chair, I chewed my fingernail. I sent back, "What if I can't?"

The question had been eating me up inside.

I stared at the screen for a moment, waiting for an answer, but nothing came. Either she didn't get the message (not likely) or Bea didn't know what to say.

Well, I supposed I should get it over with. One more time, with feeling!

I stood and faced my smaller bookshelf. On the top, I had my personal altar. It was pretty simple. Thing was, I couldn't quite bring myself to invest in expensive candelabra or velvety altar cloths when I felt like no one was listening to my desperate prayers.

Still, more than once, I'd been complimented on it by Elder

Witches. Simple was closer to the heart of the divine, they'd said.

Bea had been so jealous, and said that maybe laziness was close to the heart of the divine too.

That had been unfair. After all, despite how I might feel about the absence of real magic in my life, I'd put a lot of effort into making my altar nice. I'd made the cloth from the back of an old purple silk shirt and added some golden puff paint. After finding a Celtic knot design in a craft book of Mom's, I'd carefully cut out a stencil and painted the edges in the pattern. It was kind of cool, if you ignored the frayed bits where I hadn't gotten the hem right.

The only items I kept on the surface of the altar were three candles, an incense holder, and a small statue of Bast, the Egyptian cat goddess that Bea had bought me after our cat Mr. Snuffles died.

I stared hard at the wicks the way I'd seen Mom do, and then snapped my fingers. The room remained dark, the candles unlit.

Well, I still couldn't do that trick. To be fair, conjuring fire was an advanced spell. Even Bea couldn't do it reliably every time.

With a sigh, I removed the matches from their hiding place on the shelf behind the cloth, and lit the candles the traditional way. They glowed warmly. I took a deep breath and tried to find my "inner stillness." I had to concentrate to keep my toes from tapping and my fingers from fidgeting. But I could do it. It just took serious effort.

At last I felt a calmness settle over me, like a warm cloak.

This was the point that always gave me hope. I felt relaxed but alert. Energy hummed along points on my body, my chakras. Magic seemed imminent. I could feel it in me.

Slowly, as though not to frighten away a timid beast, I lifted my right hand. All I had to do tonight was call forth the energy of air, as part of a circle casting. Just a little breeze or shift in air pressure was the only thing I needed to conjure. My face tightened with effort as I tried to push all that hopeful stillness out into some kind of manifestation of wind.

"Come on," I whispered.

The window was open. A few minutes ago the breeze flapped the curtains playfully. Now . . . now that I needed a sign, nothing. The cloth lay ramrod straight, not even a flutter. It was almost laughable. Whatever I wanted, I swore, the universe gave me the opposite. I needed a bit of air, but I got a perfect nothing.

Hopefully, I waited for several heartbeats more. Then I finally gave up and flopped back onto the bed.

"Crap," I muttered.

The very second I gave up, the candles flickered and the curtain lifted slightly.

"It's like you mock me," I told the breeze that brought a slight, cool kiss of moisture to my cheek.

Rolling over, I looked out the window. Through the gnarled branches of the massive, ancient pine, the sky had faded to a dusty purple. A blue jay flitted onto a branch and screeched a complaining song before fluttering off again. A large shadowy something slunk across the vine-covered fence.

Wait, what?

I looked closer. There was nothing but the cedar planks and

massive, broad leaves of the hops plant that spread out of control in long, twisted vines that ran along the side of the house. No, it must have been my imagination playing tricks. No one would lurk around our house; we didn't have anything worth stealing. Besides, this was St. Paul. St. Paul might officially be a city and the capital of Minnesota, but it was much more like a sleepy little burg . . . especially after dark.

Could it be Thompson coming to toilet paper my trees or something? "Hey," I yelled out the window. "If that's you, Matt Thompson, I see you!"

But he didn't know where I lived, did he?

I didn't have time to consider that further, because Mom called cheerily up the staircase, "Time for dinner!"

"Coming," I said. Feeling like a prisoner marching to my last meal before execution, I moved slowly down the open staircase. My long, black polished nails trailed on the cherrywood.

Of course, our house was built well over a hundred years ago, and, in keeping with its advanced years, it creaked and moaned constantly. With the popping and groaning floorboards, sneaking around was next to impossible. Not that I did that—*not much*, anyway.

It's just that it would be nice, you know, occasionally, to be able to slip out the back door without anyone hearing all the hinges screeching, doors banging, and all that. Like now, for instance, it would be great to have white spongy, soft wall-to-wall carpeting like at Bea's, and one of those glass doors that slid open silently onto a pine deck, an overgrown backyard, and freedom.

"I said, are you excited for tonight?" Mom repeated, louder this time, from where she stood leaning on the banister, wooden spoon in hand.

"Huh? Sorry, I was miles away," I confessed. Like in Iowa. Anywhere but here.

"Ah, you're thinking about tonight," she said with a smile. Her eyes twinkled behind her glasses. "No need to be nervous. I know you'll do great. All the Parker girls do, you know. It's in your blood."

How many times did I have to hear that? It was destiny!

"Don't roll your eyes at me," Mom said, but she had a smile on her face to show she was teasing a bit. "Come on, dinner is on the table. I made your favorite."

My mouth watered at the tangy scent of curry.

"I even put the apples in last. That way they'll be crispy just the way you like them."

Well, Mom was trying, at least. It was sort of sweet. Impulsively, I gave her a huge hug. "I love you," I whispered intensely, though what I really wanted to say was "I'm sorry for tonight."

"I love you too, sweetie," she said, sounding a bit baffled at my sudden burst of affection. I could only hope Mom would feel the same way about me after the Initiation disaster. "Will I get a kiss if I tell you I made chocolate birthday cake for dessert?"

"Surprise?!"

"Yes," she said with a smirk. "Surprise."

Mom had changed into a T-shirt that proclaimed WITCHES DO IT SKYCLAD, which was the lamest in-joke I'd ever heard. It was like saying witches do it naked, which was what "skyclad" meant. And didn't everyone "do it" in the nude? Not that I had any real experience with that either, because, well, being a strange, geeky witch girl didn't make a person terribly popular in a high school full of cheerleaders and jocks.

I sat in my customary spot at the dining room table. I always felt a little silly sitting in the huge, cavernous room. There was a gigantic mirrored, carved buffet along the far wall. We rarely turned on the overhead light. It was a huge chandelier with a zillion bulbs, great for those parties we never hosted, but way too bright for an intimate dinner. So we ate by the illumination of a floor lamp that cast a circle of light on the corner of the table.

I spooned out a large helping of rice and smothered it with the chicken curry. "So . . . uh, about tonight," I started, but petered out, uncertain. Did I opt for the truth?

The doorbell rang.

Saved by the bell? I looked to Mom, but she had an equally confused expression on her face. "That can't be Bea," she said, checking the clock on the wall. "She knows when we're going, doesn't she? That mother of hers is always so anxious. Will you go tell her we're eating dinner?"

"Sure," I said, curious who it could be.

The bell rang again when I was halfway there. It wasn't like Bea to be quite so insistent. "I'm coming!" I shouted.

When I got there, I whipped the door open, ready to give Bea a piece of my mind. But it wasn't Bea after all. In her place stood—or, more accurately, swayed—a man I'd never seen before in my life.

He had pale-as-a-ghost skin, and haunting eyes that flicked across my face as though searching for something. He was handsome in a broody, gaunt sort of way, but he looked sick. One of his hands clutched at his side, and the other gripped the doorframe with a white-knuckle grip, like it took all his effort to remain upright.

"Anastasija?" he asked, pronouncing my full name smoothly

and gracefully, almost like music. Not like when anyone else tried.

"Yes," I answered. "Do I know you?"

"Will you let me in? I'm Alexander Ramses. I believe I'm your father."

Four

My father?

Ramses was my middle name, but . . .

I blinked unbelievingly at the pale form wobbling at the threshold. His hair was so dark it could have passed for a shadow. Much, I thought, like my own. His eyes that stared questioningly at me were the same ice-cold blue of my left iris.

But . . .

It just couldn't be my father.

"I'm sorry, I don't have a father," I explained. My voice sounded hollowly polite even to my own ears, like I was patiently putting off an encyclopedia salesman.

"I'm sure that's what you've been led to believe." His mouth quirked into a smile, but it quickly collapsed into a grimace as he clutched his side tighter. His voice sounded strained, urgent. "Tell me you haven't gone to the Initiation yet. Tell me I'm not too late."

"Too late for what?"

His intensely blue eyes gripped me in his gaze. "You have no idea, do you? She never told you." He shook his head, as though arguing with himself over some point. Then his jaw flexed. "Well, there's no time now. I'll have to explain it to you on the way."

He took my arm as though he was going to lead me out the door. I pulled back. "I'm not going anywhere with you. I don't even know who you are." Over my shoulder, I shouted for help. "Mom!"

"Your mother? Amelia? No!" the man said, clutching my arm so tightly it caused me to gasp.

"Hey. Let go of me," I insisted. Then, looking down at the hand wrapped around my forearm, I noticed the smear of black between each of his fingers. Blood? "Oh my God, are you bleeding?"

He looked down at the bloody imprint he left on my arm and quickly retracted his hand. "Yes," he said, looking behind him again into the darkness outside the still-open door. "Our enemies are gathering. You've been discovered. You cannot go to the Wiccaning. I've held them off as long as I could. But we're wasting precious time. We must go, Princess."

Princess? What was that? An awkward attempt at a term of endearment? "Go? Where? Anyway, I can't go. I've got school tomorrow."

From the other room, Mom shouted, "Who is it? Who's at the door?" I could hear her coming down the hall.

The man—Ramses, was it?—seemed to shrink back at the sound of Mom's voice, but he stood his ground. "Ana, today is your birthday, yes?"

I nodded mutely, wondering how this stranger knew. Could he really be my father?

"Sixteen on the sixteenth," he continued, his voice straining a bit. "You must forget school, forget this life. Come with me."

Luke, I am your father.

I couldn't help but laugh at the absurdity of it all. "You've got to be kidding me."

Mom's voice was closer now. "Ana? Who is that?"

Ignoring Mom for the moment, I continued to stare at the stranger in wonderment. "Go with you? Dude, I don't even know you," I said.

"A great tragedy," Ramses agreed. He put his hand to his heart and bowed his head slightly. "And, believe me, not of my choosing. But I have been with you from the beginning, my child. I am your kin."

Mom came into the hallway, saw the man, and shrieked, "Back to hell with you, demon!"

Ramses straightened himself up as best he could, given that he was dripping blood onto the hall carpeting, and said, "Amelia, you have denied our child her birthright. This violates the treaty. Anastasija should know the truth."

Yeah, this whole encounter was deeply confusing. A little explanation would go a long way. I was about to tell Mom so when I felt the atmosphere shift. Magic was afoot. "Wait, Mom," I started, but Mom interrupted.

"North, south, east, west, spiderweb shall bind him best—," Mom began intoning. I could feel power begin to swirl. The magazines and mail piled on the front-hall table began to flutter expectantly. The porch light flashed on a fluff of dust—a spider's web?—spinning through the air.

Now, why couldn't I do stuff like that?

Ramses took a step into the house, but raised his hands as

though in surrender. His eyes nervously followed the speck of fluff as it began to encircle him, a thin, white thread unraveling and growing impossibly long with each turn.

"Now, no need for any of this," he said. "Let me take the girl with me."

"Take her? Never! You have no right to lay any claim now, not after all this time." Mom broke from the spell to glare at him. The spiderweb net wobbled momentarily, as though the wind might abandon it.

"But I do, and you know it." Ramses' tone was strong, clear, and just a little fierce. "The time has come. The princess must return to her kingdom."

He didn't really just say that, did he? Was the guy insane? I felt a little faint.

Mom, however, seemed to be taking it seriously. She raised her hands, palms out. "East, west, north, south," she continued. "Hold his limbs and shut his mouth."

Wait, was Mom really casting a rhyming spell? Did those really work? I always thought that was another one of those in-jokes among witches to fool the uninitiated. Maybe I really had hexed Thompson with the rhyme about sex.

A sudden burst of wind rushed through the hall. The mail rushed out into the street, and my hair flapped wildly. The spiderweb whirled furiously, spitting out thread as it circled him faster and faster. Ramses batted at it as it tightened around his arms and legs. The more he swatted, the more entangled he became. His eyes searched me out with an imploring look, asking for my aid. But what could I do? I didn't even know if I wanted to help him, and if I did, I couldn't fight Mom's magic. I had none of my own. Anyway . . . he was just a demented stranger . . . right?

Returning his attention to Mom, he said, "You disrespect both our clans with this action, Amelia. If I must, I will send my army."

I turned, hoping to buy a clue about what he was talking about from Mom, but her expression had darkened in a way I'd never seen before. It was more than a little frightening. The windows rattled, and the air tore at my hair. The roar of the wind was deafening, and though he was trying to continue to speak, I couldn't hear a word. In fact, I had to hold on to the doorframe to keep from getting swept away myself. Miraculously, Ramses stood upright against the onslaught. He was looking more and more like a silk-wrapped mummy, however.

Mom turned her anger on me suddenly. She seemed frustrated that her magical blast hadn't been more successful. "You invited him in, didn't you?"

Had I? I didn't think I had, but I couldn't remember. Either way, I got the distinct impression that had been the wrong thing to do. "Uh, I don't know. But it's not like he's a vampire or anything."

Mom grimaced, leaving me confused. I looked at Ramses again with his jet-black hair and pale skin, pushing against the massive windstorm.

"He's not, right?"

Mom either didn't hear or chose not to answer.

A vampire?

That was fiction, wasn't it?

And if it wasn't, was I supposed to take his other claim seriously too? So I was some kind of vampire princess?

"I can't believe you invited him inside. Now I'm going to have to pull out all the stops," Mom said.

It could get worse? I'd never seen a spell this powerful, much less used as a kind of assault on another human being.

Who just might be my long-lost dad. I wasn't sure how I felt about this. I mean, shouldn't I at least get to know the guy before we kicked his ass?

Mom's power welled up, searing hot like lava, seething through the air. The air crackled with it.

"No, wait." My protest died in the noise of the maelstrom. Something inside me flickered. I felt it flutter and then die, like a candle guttered in the wind.

Mom shook out her wild curls and raised her hands again to continue the spell. "Seal his eyes and choke his breath, wrap him in the ropes of death."

And—pow!—just like that, Ramses flew off the doorstep and into the night. Mom, quite literally, kicked the guy to the curb. My mouth hung open. I'd never seen Mom quite so ninja-witchy.

In fact, I always figured this kind of violent spell was, you know, black magic, the stuff good witches stayed away from.

Meanwhile, Ramses lay crumpled there on the neighbor's boulevard, not moving, completely cocooned in webbing. He looked like a giant cotton ball. Was he okay? I mean, I probably shouldn't care, but . . .

As if possessed by a mind of its own, my foot started out the door. Mom grabbed my shoulder, stopping me cold.

"But he's hurt," I protested, my eyes flicking to the mummy-white blob nervously. What if he really was my dad? I tried to shake Mom's grip, but it tightened like a vise. "He could die!"

"I should hope so." Mom's tone was icy cold. She adjusted her glasses, as though to better inspect her handiwork.

"What?" I ripped myself out from Mom's restraining hand. No way did Mom mean that! Screw her, I thought. He didn't seem all that threatening. Okay, so he wanted to take me away, but did he really deserve to be all gummed up like one of Spider-Man's villains? I was going to help him.

Mom reached around me and slammed the door shut with an ominous bang.

"You have done enough damage, young lady."

"But I didn't invite him in, I swear," I said, fairly sure it was the truth.

"You must have."

I frowned because Mom seemed so sure I had, and I was more and more convinced I hadn't. It didn't really matter. What mattered was that Ramses was okay out there.

I tried the door, but I knew it was useless. I'd already felt Mom use her magic to turn the lock. "Why won't you let me help him?"

"Because it's not safe," Mom said simply, firmly. I opened my mouth to protest, but Mom cut me off. "He's . . . really hard to damage. You're going to have to trust me on this one."

Trust her? Ms. Never-says-a-word? Oh, there was so much that I could say about that, but I hardly knew where to start, and given Mom's mood, I was a little bit afraid of ending up co-cooned myself. Yet, despite my better judgment, everything just bubbled over. "What just happened? He said he was my father and all sorts of crazy stuff, like I'm some kind of princess. Was he for real?"

"I still can't believe you let him in over the threshold. Now we have to up the wards," Mom continued, completely ignoring my questions. She put her palms flat on the wood of the door.

"Wards? Seriously?" Did Mom really mean what she seemed to be implying? Did an invitation really matter?

"You broke it. Help me fix it." Mom waited expectantly at the door until I joined her in the same position.

Mom closed her eyes, and I tried to conjure my stillness. But it was much harder than usual, with all the questions running through my head. I mean, WTF? If Ramses wasn't my dad, Mom wasn't doing a great job at denying it. In fact, standing here upping the wards like he was some kind of threat . . . well, that just made this whole crazy event that much more plausible.

I sneaked a peek at Mom. Her eyes were closed the way they often were when she concentrated on magic, but I could see tension creasing the corners of her mouth.

Mom's magic flowed out into the door. It quickly surrounded the entire house in a kind of protective bubble. Jealously, I sensed the texture and strength of Mom's magic. Instead of wind, this energy felt more solid, like earth. I could smell something, like loam or moss, ancient and intense. Mom whispered something in Latin, a language she saved for only the most powerful spells.

She shook herself out and straightened her shirt. "Well done." She patted me on the shoulder, like I'd been of some help. "Well, we should probably finish dinner before it gets cold."

Dinner? Who could think of food right now? I looked at Mom like she was insane. Totally casually, like nothing had happened, she headed back to the kitchen.

I stood at the door, stunned into inaction. Two seconds later, my mouth started up. "Was that really my dad? And did you seriously just wrap him in a spiderweb and leave him on the curb like the recycling?"

The clank of dishes.

Finally, Mom replied, "I don't want to talk about it."

No surprise there.

Cautiously, I moved aside the heavy lace curtain that covered the window nearest the door. Though it was still dark, an old-fashioned streetlamp illuminated the neighbor's boulevard. Shreds of white fluff were scattered on the neatly manicured lawn. There was no sign of . . . I wasn't sure what to call him anymore. It was beginning to seem like he was more than just some stranger who'd happened to show up on my birthday. But it wasn't as if I knew him enough, really, to call him Dad. I settled on Ramses. It was the name we shared, after all.

Still. Seeing the shreds of cottony fluff sent relief sighing through my nerves. Maybe he was okay after all. Then I tensed again as I wondered, what of the people he'd said attacked him? Could they have carried him away?

"Who do you think is after Dad?" I decided I'd call Ramses Dad when talking to Mom. It was sure to annoy her. "And what did he mean when he said I shouldn't go to the Initiation? Do you think someone will try to sabotage it or something?"

There was a long silence from the kitchen, and I dared to hope Mom was actually considering an answer instead of more evasion. But all she said was, "Your curry is getting cold."

"Yeah, and this avoidance is getting really old," I shot back, gearing up for a fight.

The foyer was dark, and the light from the kitchen glowed brightly. At first, I wondered if Mom had heard me, but then I detected the soft sounds of sobbing.

Mom crying? The fight in me instantly deflated at the sound. Mom never cried. Surely this was one of the seven signs of the apocalypse. I rushed into the kitchen.

Mom sat with elbows leaning heavily on the counter, her head buried in her hands. Her shoulders trembled. I reached out a tentative, awkward hand and placed it on Mom's back. I wanted to say something that would make Mom stop that pitiful sobbing, but all I had were questions that I was sure would upset her.

Mom sniffed deeply. Lifting her glasses, she scrubbed at her face to wipe off the tears. "What an awful night."

And the smell coming now from the oven could only be my cake burning. I rushed over to switch off the heat. The fire alarm started beeping. I wrenched open the door with the oven mitts.

"Oh, no," Mom sobbed, looking at the blackened heap I pulled from the oven. "Your cake."

⟍⟋ *Five*

"**S**urprise!" I said with a little smile, setting the mess on the burners.

"I'm so sorry," Mom said. "For everything."

That sounded awfully meaningful, so I waited for the rest. Mom sat down dejectedly on the nearby stool and said nothing more. I leaned against the counter. The room had gotten hot and stinky. I wiped my brow with the quilted cotton mitt. "We could skip the Initiation," I suggested. It was going to suck anyway. "I mean, if you're not up for it. And Dad said—"

Straightening suddenly, Mom shook herself out and stared at me fiercely like she might deny that the man at the door was, in fact, my father.

I held my breath. Maybe I'd finally get some answers.

Instead, Mom sniffed. "Don't be ridiculous. The Initiation is more critical than ever now. You should eat. You can't do magic on an empty stomach."

"Look, Mom, I can't do magic at all." I wasn't hungry anymore, but I knew better than to argue when Mom was in a mood like this. I followed her back into the dining room to sit. "I'm not sure eating is going to help."

"Don't be silly. Your teachers say you'll do fine if you apply yourself."

"I apply myself plenty," I said, wanting to talk about what had just happened, not this. I pushed the congealing curry sauce around the edges of my plate. "I work really hard, Mom. The fact is I suck."

"Don't use language like that. And stop tearing yourself down. You're just experiencing a little stage fright. It's very natural," Mom snapped. Then softening, she smiled. "It's never as bad as you think. I remember my first time performing magic in a public circle. . . ."

Shamelessly, I tuned out. Mom was making an effort to mend bridges and all that, but I'd heard this particular story more times than I could count, and honestly, it wasn't helpful right now. What I really wanted to talk about was Ramses. I glanced out the window, secretly hoping to see him skulking around. Alas, in the darkness, all I could really see was the reflection of the interior, and my own wistful expression.

Seeing myself, I thought maybe I did notice a hint of familiarity in our features. Mom tanned easily. My own face was as ghostly pale as . . . Ramses'.

Who was he? And what had he meant by "princess"? It sounded kind of romantic, like some sort of special inheritance. Or was he being metaphoric? He couldn't really have meant to imply I was some kind of royalty, like with a castle and stuff, could he? And with an army? Was he a lunatic or . . . what?

A vampire.

Did vampires have kids? Was that even possible?

I desperately wanted to ask Mom, but I knew I'd only get stonewalled. So, for the moment, I satisfied myself with eating the curry. It was quite good. The apples had gotten a bit soggy and the sauce chilled, but the spices were delicious sweet-hot. Exactly right! In three bites, my nose started to run.

"Are you even listening?" Mom asked after I failed to laugh at some joke or other.

"Not really," I said with a little smile to soften the truth. "I was thinking about that guy. Ramses? My dad? You know, the one at the door that you blasted into next week? That I wasn't supposed to have invited in? Why was that again?"

"All our wards were negated when you invited him in. The house recognized him as 'friend,' not 'foe.'"

That wasn't the real reason. I could sense it. The wards were minor magic—everyone knew that. A "pot o' protection" didn't do much to stop anyone who really wanted to cross the threshold. Besides, no one set wards too strongly. When you did that, the mail carrier couldn't find you, your friends drove by, and the house virtually disappeared or, at best, seemed abandoned. There was no way my little invitation could matter that much, if I'd even given it, especially since the wards were so inconsequential to begin with.

"Was that my dad?"

"We should probably put the dishes in the sink and get ready. Bea will be here any minute."

I stared pointedly at Mom's smiling face, and added, "He's different than I expected. I mean, the way you never talk about him, I kind of thought maybe he'd died, you know, or something tragic like that."

"His death would hardly be tragic," Mom said as she reached for my plate to stack on her own. "And he is dead."

What? Did she mean . . . ?

"To me," Mom added quickly. "To the world. He shouldn't be here."

My breath caught. It was the first ever acknowledgment that my dad existed. But what did it mean? "To the world? How do you figure that?"

"I do *not* want to talk about it," Mom reiterated as she turned her back to me to put the dishes in the sink.

The doorbell made us jump. I got up. "Maybe it's him again!"

"*I'll* check," Mom said firmly, but I followed anyway.

Together we crept toward the front door. Mom sidled up to the window and pulled aside the curtain. I peeked around her shoulder. Illuminated in the porch light was Bea, who was staring at the house, frowning. Bea still had her hair up in pigtails, but she'd changed into "serious" witch clothing: a turtleneck, jeans, and a leather jacket.

"It's only Bea," Mom said, and I heard her let out a relieved breath.

Once the door was opened and hugs went around, Bea pointed to the ceiling and asked, "What's up with the super wards? Mom almost drove right past the house. And a spider exploded on your porch."

"Sorry," Mom said. "We had an unexpected guest."

"My dad," I supplied.

"Seriously!" Bea squealed, taking my hands. "What was he like?"

"Well, kind of younger than I would have expected." I slid

my eyes over to Mom, who frowned so deeply lines showed on her face.

Bea's smile was wide and mischievous.

"He's older than he looks," Mom said gruffly.

More confirmation? I felt my face pale; it *really* was my dad!

Mom sensed her tactical error and gave an irritated wave in the direction of the staircase. "You should get dressed, Ana. We're going to be late."

Bea and I scooted up the stairs before Mom could waylay Bea and keep us from gossiping. Once upstairs, I quickly shut the door.

Bea flicked on a lamp on the nightstand, and then flopped dramatically onto the quilted bedspread. "Tell me everything!"

Opening the door of the closet, I started rummaging through my clothes. I pulled out a dress and showed it to Bea, who shook her head. "Well." I shrugged. "It was weird. You know, I always thought he might be dead. We never hear from him. Now that it's my birthday, he just sort of showed up. And . . . I think he was hurt. He didn't want me to go to the Initiation. Mom yelled at him and wrapped him in a spiderweb."

"What? Seriously?"

"Yeah." I paused to lean against the closet door. "She used a spell I'd never heard of and suddenly Ramses—uh, that's Dad— was all mummified. He never got a chance to say more than boo. Well, actually, he managed to say stuff, but nothing that made sense. He said all sorts of crazy things about enemies and armies and blood claims. I don't know. Honestly, it's really hard to take it all in."

"Do you think, you know, he was high or something?"

The thought hadn't occurred to me. It didn't seem right,

though. I shook my head. "He was wounded. Bleeding from a cut on his side." I lifted my arm to show her the smear. Bea gasped excitedly and jumped up to examine me.

"We've got to wash this off!" A note of horror crept into her voice as she dragged me off to the bathroom.

As she lathered, rinsed, and repeated my arm, it occurred to me that I supposed I should have freaked out more. A strange man bled all over me. Not cool.

But I could hardly unravel any of it, much less work up concern over infectious-disease control. My head was spinning. I still didn't even really know who that guy had been. Was he my dad? Really? And was my dad a vampire? Or insane? Or both?

Bea looked at me, her eyes searching. "What kind of person shows up at someone's house bleeding?"

Someone not normal. The implication was obvious in Bea's tone. Yeah. I could hardly argue with *that*. Vampire or not, the guy was weird. I grabbed a towel and carefully wiped my arm.

Bea watched me with a kind of sad look, like she felt sorry for me. Was it because she thought my dad was some kind of homeless crazy guy or . . . no, Bea would never keep a secret like this from me. Would she?

"So, what did he look like?"

We made our way back to my bedroom as I considered what to say. Once there, I busied myself with returning the dress to the hanger, and then choosing a black silk blouse. I held the blouse up to my chest and checked my look in the full-length mirror on the closet door. My reflection was pale and skinny, but the shirt swished in a way that at least showed off what few curves

I possessed. Still, it looked a bit dowdy. I pulled out my sparkly halter top.

"He was pale." I touched my own face in memory. Ugh, you could almost see the veins at my temple. I brushed my bangs to cover them. Pointing to my blue eye, I said, "His eyes were like this one."

"Was he tall? Handsome?"

I gave her a you-gross-me-out expression. "I didn't notice that stuff. I mean, he might be my dad, you know?"

"You're not sure that he's your dad?"

I shrugged. "I'm pretty sure, but, you know, Mom won't confirm or deny. . . . What am I supposed to think?" I pulled off my shirt, and I wiggled into the halter top. When I put the blouse over the top, the combination was serious enough for the ritual, but looked a bit sexy too.

"You look outstanding," Bea said sincerely. Bea tended toward voluptuousness, and, of course, always admired my stick figure. Meanwhile, I wished I were more curvaceous, like Bea. Bea stood and threw her arms around me and smiled at our reflections. "Like a witch without her hat."

"Speaking of a perfect accessory, I almost forgot this." I grabbed her necklace from where I'd looped it over my dresser mirror. The beads tingled warmly against my skin. The goddess figurine slid into the hollow between my breasts.

"Perfect," Bea said.

We admired ourselves for a moment until I broke the mood by asking, "You know tonight is going to suck, right?"

"No, I'm telling you. My aunt Diane had a dream. Tonight is going to be remembered forever." Bea's aunt Diane was a well-known clairvoyant dreamer in the coven. It was rare her dreams didn't come true.

"That doesn't mean it's going to go well," I reminded Bea. "It could be remembered for being the most awfulest ever."

"You know, your mom might be right. You do need a shot of self-confidence. You have to remember, Ana: you're one of us. The family. The goddess doesn't abandon her own."

What about my other half—the half that came from my dad? But I kept my mouth shut, and nodded. "Yeah, I suppose a miracle could occur."

"Now you're talking," Bea said.

LUCKILY, BEA KEPT UP A constant chatter in the backseat, because the car ride to the covenstead was awkward.

Mom had changed into a lovely full-length dress I'd never seen before. It was emerald green velvet and had long, droopy sleeves and gold embroidering like something out of medieval times. I tried to compliment her on it, but Mom turned the simple words into an argument about clothes.

Mom complained that I should have chosen something more befitting the seriousness of the occasion. I thought I had, and then grumbled about how there really was no point, since the whole thing was going to go to hell anyway.

For some reason, mentioning "hell" *really* set Mom off, and she hadn't spoken since.

Maybe Ramses was the Prince of Hell.

"My mom sends her regards, by the way," Bea said from the back.

That was the other elephant in the room, or car, as the case might be. Bea's mom wasn't part of the Inner Circle of the coven. She'd failed *her* Initiation. Just like I was about to.

"I wish it wasn't against the rules for your mom to come," I said kindly. What must it be like for her? All the members of Bea's family were big muckety-mucks in the coven except her mom. Even Bea's dad would be there, since he was an Elder and a high priest.

"Tonight is only for True Witches," Mom said.

I shot her a hard look. That dig wasn't necessary. And would she be so unkind when her own daughter was relegated to the Outer Court?

"Mom made an awesome treat for the cakes and ale," Bea said, totally ignoring both the cruelty and the pity. "Papa took it with him, when he went to set up."

"Oh, I love your mom's cooking!" I said honestly, happy to pick up the cue to change the subject. Bea's mom might not be Inner Circle, but she was a kitchen witch bar none. "What did she make?"

"Little savory pies. Enough for everyone, with vegetarian, vegan, nondairy, and gluten-free options!"

Bea and I laughed. It was a private joke. We always found all the different food restrictions amusing. Bea had once teased that witches like to make something for everyone, even the people who kept kosher!

"I don't know what you find so funny. That's a lot of work your mother put in," Mom said humorlessly from the driver's seat.

Boy, Mom was in a bad mood. How long until we arrived? I checked the dashboard clock: ten more minutes. The city was long behind us, and the car rolled along darkened cornfields, their tall stalks stiff and straight in perfect rows. Dark sky stretched overhead, twinkling with a multitude of stars. The moon rose full and round in the east.

"It couldn't be a more perfect night," I said. It had been cold and rainy just the day before, but today the clouds broke. The temperature of the evening air was cool, maybe sixty degrees. I'd brought along a cape to drape over my shoulders, but I wondered if I'd need it after all.

"Martha always makes the weather just right for the Initiation," Mom said with a smile. Martha was the coven's weather witch. In the Circle they called her "Grandmother Storm," because it was rumored she once conjured a great storm after a long drought. "I wonder what your gift will be, Ana."

Along with casting the circle, the initiates were expected to receive a kind of magical calling tonight, a special skill that they would develop while working in the coven. Bea hoped to be a diviner, since she loved working with astrology and tarot cards so much.

Honestly? What I wanted more than anything was simple. I wanted my name to be written in the great book. Everyone had said having an Initiation on my birthday would be so fortunate. I just wanted to survive it without too much embarrassment for everyone involved.

"Yeah, I wonder," I said wistfully. "Did you get what you wanted, Mom?"

Instantly, I knew I'd said something wrong again. By the light of the dash, I saw Mom's lips tighten. "No," she said simply. "Not entirely."

Bea and I exchanged a look. What do you suppose that meant? Bea opened her mouth as though to ask, but I shook my head in warning. Best not to push her. Mom revealed secrets only by accident.

We rode the rest of the way in silence, each lost in her own thoughts. I watched the fields roll by, which, after a turn to the left, quickly became tangled woods. We were nearly there! Shadows of oak and maple darkened the road, and Mom flicked on her high beams, watchful for rabbit or deer. Slowing the car, we scanned for the turnoff, which was easy to miss, thanks to the trees and the warding. I spotted it first. "There," I said, pointing, as Mom smoothly guided the car onto an unpaved dirt road that was little more than tire tracks.

I loved the covenstead. Most of it was undeveloped, except a small cabin near a swampy lake. I'd spent many happy summer days in my childhood wandering the forest and swimming in the mucky water, sort of like some people did at their "cabins up north." Except my cabin belonged to about twelve families, all of whom used it for recreation and, most often, for magic.

The night seemed darker the deeper we drove into the coven's property. Tall trees crowded the border of the narrow path, and occasionally a branch of an overgrown bush scraped noisily against the car's frame. The air felt expectant and heavy, like just before rain.

Something whitish flashed through the woods, as though at a gallop. I thought it might be the tail of a deer, so I said, "Slow down. There's a buck or something out there."

Mom put her foot on the brake, and we all scanned the forest. Hitting a deer could crack a radiator or worse. On top of potentially wrecking the car, there was the fact that killing a deer would be a very inauspicious beginning to the Initiation.

"Are you sure?" Mom asked after a moment of agonizingly slow progress. "I don't see anything."

Whatever it had been was long gone. "It must have really been cruising," I said. "There's no sign of it now."

Mom brought the car up to speed, such as it was on the narrow passage. I recognized the stand of birch trees ahead; we were almost to the bend in the road that would bring the covenstead in view.

I hugged myself in the dim interior of the car. This was it. The big night. Bea and I had imagined this so many times; my heart began to race with anticipation. Just ahead, the woods opened to a clearing that was littered with cars. We bumped along the uneven grass to find an empty spot. Scanning the vehicles, I noted familiar bumper stickers and license plates. It looked like almost everyone was here already.

"Oh, I'm so excited," Bea said, bouncing happily in her seat in the back.

Even Mom cracked a smile. "You girls will do great. I just know it."

"Did Aunt Diane tell you about her dream?" Bea asked Mom. "This year will be memorable."

Mom gave me a proud, anxious look. "I hope she's right."

"Memorable doesn't necessarily mean good," I reminded everyone quietly as Mom pulled the car into an empty spot between a large oak stump and a dusty white van.

"Stop being such a pessimist," Bea said with a broad smile. "It's going to be great."

I still wasn't convinced, but Bea's enthusiasm was infectious. I could feel myself smiling back, despite my worries. Once out of the car, Bea grabbed my hand with a giggle. She pulled me, bounding, to the back door of the cabin. I couldn't help but laugh along.

The covenstead was built by hand sometime in the 1970s. Everything about it was very "back to the land," from its rough-hewn exterior to the broad, communal floor plan. We let ourselves in and slipped our shoes off in the mudroom, which was really not much more than a long hallway with a few benches and pegs on the wall for hanging coats. There were several dozen shoes and coats already piled around, and we could hear the murmur of voices and laughter in the living room.

"I wonder if Nikolai is here." Bea twirled her pigtails as she whispered in my ear.

I rolled my eyes. He was supercute and everything, but I didn't quite understand why Bea got all weak-kneed around him. Maybe it was the band thing. Rockers always had a big appeal for Bea. Of course, who was I kidding? If I thought I had a chance with him, I'd be all over that. "We're a bit late, though not quite on 'pagan time' yet," I said, but Bea was already out of her shoes and into the living room to find out.

I took my time, slowly untying my Converses. Despite my growing enthusiasm, I remembered Ramses' words of warning.

Just then, Mom came in, carrying a grocery bag of supplies from the trunk. "Oh," Mom said, seeing me sitting on the bench. "I thought you'd be mingling by now. You're not still nervous, are you?"

"Why won't you talk to me about Dad? Is he really that horrible?" Despite myself, my voice trembled.

Setting the bag down by the door, Mom slid onto the bench next to me. She put an arm around my shoulder and let out a heavy sigh. "I suppose I do owe you some explanation. After all, in a matter of hours you'll be a full member of this coven and all our secrets will be yours to keep as well."

I could hardly believe my ears. I held my breath.

"Your father isn't one of us. He's from the other side. Our union—him and me—well, it was meant to be a peace treaty of sorts, but it was a mistake from the beginning."

Six

A mistake? Did she mean me?

Mom saw my expression and shook her head. "It's very important that before I tell you more, you pass your Initiation. You see, your father is at the center of all this, and I'm so angry at him for showing up tonight and putting crazy thoughts into your head. You need to focus on the Initiation. Try to put him out of your mind for now, okay? I promise it will all make sense soon."

It was disappointingly vague, but I nodded. "You promise you'll tell me?"

"Witch to witch," Mom said, giving me a hand to shake.

I hesitated before taking Mom's offered palm. "And if I don't become a True Witch tonight?"

"Honey, you will. Blood will out."

The second mention of blood tonight, and I felt even more uncertain as I shook on Mom's solemn oath. "Witch to witch," I repeated.

Mom gave me a quick hug and a gentle push in the direction of the living room. "I heard Nikolai would be here." She smiled. "I think he likes you."

"Mom!" I admonished, and I felt myself color with embarrassment. Besides, Bea would be so miffed if she thought that was true. To escape Mom's sly, knowing smile, I hurried off to the crowded common room.

I DIDN'T LIKE THESE BIG gatherings. Even though I knew everyone here, I never quite knew what to do with myself. Bea could insert herself into a group without seeming rude or awkward. Not me. I just stood near the fireplace and watched with some jealousy as Bea moved from group to group easily. Finally, Bea caught my eye and waved me over.

Of course, she would have to be standing next to Nikolai when she did.

He brightened when he saw me approaching, and I had to admit he had a dazzling smile. Plus, thanks to a Russian father and Romany mother, he had thick, dark curls and a kind of smoldering intensity that both frightened and enchanted me. Like the rest of us, he'd dressed the part of the young witch. In his case, he opted for the billowy peasant shirt with poet sleeves and tight leather pants. Wow, he looked good in those. The motorcycle boots were a nice, modern touch, especially with the ankle jewelry jangling like spurs near his heels.

I had some trouble meeting his eyes by the time I stood next to Bea, who thoughtfully widened the circle to include me. The other person in their group was Shannon, who was not yet fifteen. She had tinsel woven into her tight cornrows and glitter on her cheeks. Shannon was the opposite of me in many ways—baby plump, dark skinned—but the biggest was that she was a prodigy: so good at magic that she'd be Initiated early, almost two years ahead of schedule.

"Did you see Nik's new ink?" Shannon giggled excitedly. "Show her! It's totally awesome. I can't wait until I'm eighteen and I can get a tattoo."

Nikolai raised his sleeve to the bicep to show off a band of intertwined blue and green dragons. Where it was decorated, his skin looked rough and raised and I noted a tiny scab over one of the darker lines. "Ow," I said sympathetically. "I bet that hurt."

"Ha! You owe me twenty bucks," Nikolai told Bea.

"It's a technicality," Bea said with a faux pout. "She might not have *asked* if it hurt, but she still mentioned it."

"Yeah, but I told you she wouldn't be cliché." Nikolai gave me an approving glance, as though he expected me to generally perform above average. I struggled not to blush furiously at his attention. Turning back to Bea, he added, "I say you owe me."

"Fine, you'll just have to come over to my house and collect it after school," Bea purred. Could she be more obviously flirting? I tried to catch Shannon's eye so we could talk about something else, but Shannon had that same adoring look riveted completely on Nikolai.

"My mom would never let me have a tattoo," Shannon said. "You're so lucky."

"My dad thinks only gang members and prisoners get tattoos," Nikolai said with a shrug. "But my mom is cool with it."

"I wish my mom was a Gypsy," Shannon said.

"Romany," three of us corrected in unison, and we all

laughed, even Shannon, after she grimaced a little "oopsie" face.

"Hey," Nikolai said with a shy smile. "Happy birthday, Ana. I got you something. Remind me to give it to you, after."

My blush deepened. "Uh, thanks."

"Yeah, happy birthday," Shannon added quickly.

I thanked everyone, and we all fell into an awkward kind of silence.

"So here we are," Bea said conspiratorially. "The Four."

We all looked at one another in turn. During the ceremony, we'd represent the four directions, the four elements, and the four winds. I would be east and represent air and new beginnings, Bea would be the fiery south with her flirtatious passion, Nikolai would be west's deep mysterious water, and Shannon would anchor us all in earth in the north.

"Are you guys ready?" Nikolai asked. "I am so psyched."

While everyone else nodded, I didn't know what to say. At least since things started with me in the east, it'd be over quickly. I hated to ruin everyone's big night, but at least they could retake the test next year. I felt especially bad for Nik. His Initiation had already been delayed because he was getting some sort of special training from his folks' people.

"Ana? What's wrong?" Nikolai's soft voice cut through my tangled thoughts.

Before I could answer, Bea interrupted, "Her dad showed up tonight."

"What? No way!" Nikolai and Shannon shouted in surprise, and then began to bombard me with questions: "Seriously?" "What was he like?" "Is he here?" "Is he a witch?" "What did your mom do?"

Luckily, before I could even begin to formulate a response, the bell that called the meeting to order rang out. We all hushed and turned toward the center of the room where the high priestess stood. Tonight, the high priestess would be Bea's aunt Diane, who seemed to look directly at me when she said, "I dreamed of tonight. It will be auspicious for these young people, and we shouldn't keep them waiting any longer. We'll set up in the grove. . . ."

Diane continued spelling out the administrative things she needed done—where people would stand, what things needed to be preplaced, and where. I knew it all already by heart, and I found myself watching Diane as she talked. Diane was a stout woman, the sort people always said looked as though they came from "sturdy, peasant stock." Her steel gray hair was cut short. Tonight she wore a simple black button-down shirt and matching jeans that didn't do much to flatter her gender-neutral, squarish figure. She would have looked severe and decidedly unfriendly had it not been for her quick and easy laugh. Diane found so much humor in the world that she was rarely without a broad smile or a deep, explosive belly laugh. She was a kind and fair teacher, if demanding. I always really liked Diane, even though, at first, I'd been scared of her gruff exterior.

I was glad that Diane would be the one officiating this disaster. If anyone could potentially salvage it, it would be her.

Now Diane was waving everyone off to their respective assignments. After a noisy exodus, the five of us remained in the room. Diane came up to the circle of friends, and gave each a soft smile. "Okay," she said. "I want you all to take a moment to meditate before you take your positions in the circle. The Initiation is more than just a test. It's a coming of age. When we are finished tonight, you will be transformed into witches of the coven—full members with all the benefits and responsibilities that entails. While you're meditating, I want you to consider what you will contribute to our group. When you're ready, come out with an open and willing heart."

"In perfect love and perfect trust," the four of us intoned with a weighty seriousness.

Diane laughed. "Remember to have fun too."

"Thanks, Auntie Diane." Bea smiled.

"Yeah, thanks," the rest of us agreed, though my voice was softer and more nervous than the others'.

Diane seemed to sense my hesitation and caught my eye. She put a hand on my shoulder and gave it a quick, reassuring squeeze. "Nothing ever goes exactly as planned. Make your own destiny."

I frowned in mild confusion. That was certainly a strange thing to say for a pep talk. "Uh, okay."

With a nod to everyone, Diane swept out the sliding glass door with a flourish, leaving us on our own.

"What's with the destiny thing?" Bea asked, jealousy creeping into her voice.

"Shhh," Shannon admonished, bowing her head. "We're supposed to be meditating."

"I'm sure she meant that for everyone," Nikolai said. "She just happened to be looking at Ana."

"You guys, you're breaking my concentration," Shannon said, moving away from the group to stand on the other side of the built-in stone fireplace.

"Sorry. Jeez, who knew you needed absolute silence to concentrate? I thought you were supposed to be some kind of magical genius," Bea said, though her eyes stayed locked on me.

I just wanted to shrink away from this whole affair, so I said, "I meditate better outside. I'm just going to step out onto the porch." Before anyone could protest, I went to the back hall and grabbed my shoes. Without even bothering to put them on, I slipped through the glass door and closed it behind me.

Once outside, I let out a long, slow breath. The glow from the interior electric lights cast soft yellow light on the wide, cedar planking of the deck. A few patio chairs rested against the wall, and I plopped into one and pulled on my tennies.

Bea could be so jealous, and of the stupidest stuff. Honestly, I would happily exchange places and let Bea be the one with all the so-called "destiny" hanging over her head. Why had Diane said that, anyway? Had she dreamed something specifically about me after all? And did it have anything to do with Ramses showing up?

As if tonight needed more complications.

Once my shoes were laced, I got up to lean on the railing. The wood creaked, startling a rabbit from its hidey spot in the peonies underneath. The bright white of its cottontail quickly disappeared into the thick forest.

Was that a good omen?

Honestly, I didn't know much about animal totems. It really wasn't my area of expertise. Nikolai would know, though. I thought about going in and asking him, but when I glanced back at the cabin, I could see that he and Bea were holding hands, their heads bowed. Trust Bea to find a way to meditate *and* flirt!

Turning back toward the night, I glanced up at the sky. The

moon rose just above the line of trees. Its cool, subtle light cast a silvery edge on everything. Magic filled the air; I could sense it. Maybe everyone was right. Perhaps I shouldn't be so doom and gloom. Just because my powers had never manifested before didn't mean they wouldn't tonight, did it? The rabbit might be a good sign after all. Weren't bunnies supposed to be all about fertility? Maybe some wild seed would sprout inside me right now, at this instant, and everything would actually work out perfectly.

Anything was possible, right?

It's not like I didn't believe in magic.

Thus buoyed, I skipped down the short flight of stairs and headed for the trail that led to the glen. I was as ready for the Initiation as I'd ever be. Tall grasses tugged at my jeans, and within steps of the cabin the woods became dark. I slapped at a mosquito and stumbled over a tree root. Just when I thought I should head back to the cabin for a flashlight and bug spray, I spotted a candle in a glass bowl. It floated like a flower, shedding shimmering, delicate light on the path. Two more steps revealed another.

It was a beautiful effect. I smiled when I reached a curve in the path that was slightly elevated and could see the trail of flickering lights leading to a natural opening among the trees.

Once within the circle of trees, I saw that candles had been placed in a large circle. The coveners stood in single file around the inner edge, a circle within a circle within a circle. Everyone whose eyes met mine smiled warmly and encouragingly. Mom gave me a nod and a proud look. The person standing closest to me stepped aside, and I jumped over the candle barrier and made my way into my designated spot. A larger, unlit candle had been placed at each of the exact cardinal directions. I found the one in the east, and picked up the little book of matches with trembling hands. Diane stood in the center of the circle and gave me a broad wink.

My stomach twisted in knots. I concentrated on taking slow, deep breaths and going over the words I would say in my head. I hadn't memorized anything specific—I wasn't supposed to. But there was a sort of order to the ritual that involved welcoming the spirits of the air, and listing some of the qualities that I wanted to invoke for the purpose of the Initiation. But nothing stayed firmly in my head for very long, and I found myself shaking even harder by the time the others made their way along the wooded path to the glen.

Bea looked very poised and pleasantly aware of the eyes on her. Nikolai took his place with a subdued seriousness, while Shannon hopped on the balls of her feet with barely contained exuberance. I slapped at a mosquito that lit on my shirtsleeve, and tried not to barf.

Diane cleared her throat. "We are gathered here tonight on this full moon to bear witness to a momentous transformation." Her voice was clear, and she turned slowly in place to address everyone in the circle. "Tonight novices will become one with the coven, and be True Witches in their own right. Tonight these novices will come into their power. So mote it be."

"So mote it be," replied the coven in unison.

Bea's dad, who was acting the part of the high priest, picked up his broom from where it lay on the ground beside him and began symbolically sweeping the edges of the circle. He moved in a counterclockwise direction, and said, "I banish negative energy from this circle." Occasionally, as he moved past someone, he'd take an extra moment to mime brushing them off. Bea's dad could read auras and could tell when someone was carrying extra negativity. In his day job he was a computer programmer. Other than the thick glasses and bushy beard he wore, you couldn't tell. He biked to work every day, and had a trim, athletic body, which was currently covered in a dark, hand-sewn tunic and jeans.

When Bea's dad got to where I stood in the east, he batted furiously at the air, as though trying to chase off a hoard of bad energy. Very self-conscious that it was my bad attitude he was battling, I tried to help by clearing my mind and centering. Closing my eyes, I drew on my inner stillness until, finally, he continued around the circle. I noticed he stopped and worked furiously at each direction, though not nearly with such animation as he had by me.

All too soon he returned to his place and it was time to begin.

I took a steadying breath, and my eyes scanned the coven and the woods beyond. In the oak trees that lined the circle, I thought I saw movement. Yes, definitely. I saw it again, a flash, almost as if there was someone waving at me, trying to get my attention. I squinted until I was almost certain that someone squatted in the branches of the trees, watching the proceedings with penetrating, unearthly eyes. In fact, there seemed to be a number of someones lurking just outside the circle. I thought I could hear their panting breath, like wolves just beyond the fold.

Others seemed to sense it too. Nikolai suddenly twisted his neck to look over his shoulder, up into the branches. Someone in the circle stifled a gasp. Diane raised her hands as though to remind everyone to focus on the Initiation. "The circle is not yet cast," she said with a note of urgency in her voice. Until the circle was complete, we weren't safe from outside magical attack. I thought Diane must sense the others' presence too. With a look to me, she said, "Let us begin."

I shook out a match from the box. I struck the head, and the flame flared for a second, then blew out. I tried again. The next one went out a moment after it lit as well.

A dark chuckle echoed through the treetops.

Whatever was out there was mocking me. I tried again, and the light disappeared in a puff. My hands shook so hard, the matches spilled out of the box into the low grass, wet with dew. Now they'd never start!

I should probably just say the words and forget trying to get the candle going, but I knelt down and felt around until I found one. Everyone was watching me, even whatever hovered just outside the light of the circle in the trees.

"Welcome, east," I croaked, my voice cracking with tension.

Just then, as though by my command, all the candles went out with a whoosh. The circle was plunged into darkness.

~~— Seven

I n the sudden darkness, someone let out a bloodcurdling scream. I flinched. The coven's coherence began to disintegrate as people tried to figure out what was happening. No one left the circle, though. Instead, as if by silent cue, everyone turned to face the woods and locked hands. Diane started up the circle song: "We are a circle, within a circle, with no beginning and never ending."

The coven picked up the words; the song grew louder, more confident.

Something in the woods hooted sarcastically.

I didn't know what to do. I looked to Diane, but the high priestess was busily concentrating on keeping everyone focused on holding off the outside threat, whatever it was. Bea caught my eye and, with an uplifted chin, urged me to try calling the element again.

My fingers fumbled for a match.

"Forget that," Nikolai said, shouting to be heard over the

singing. "Let the moon be our light. Just say the words. Draw the wind. Kick a little magical ass."

Diane nodded encouragingly.

Straightening, I stood and faced the east. It was almost impossible to find my calm center when I could see the others, the shadowy things, pacing through the woods and hiding among the branches of the thick trees. Their shape seemed human, but not much else about them did. Tall and powerful figures, they snarled and snapped like animals. Who were they? Some kind of weird gang? Or were they the enemy that Mom spoke of, the ones from the "other side" that the coven was at war with?

"Come on," whined Shannon nervously. "We need to have a circle. Now."

I let the familiarity of the repetitive circle song settle my nerves. "Welcome, east," I said, as loudly as my trembling voice would allow. "Guardian of word, make our thoughts manifest."

And here was where a little puff of wind would go very nicely. I tried to magically induce a little "oomph," but, despite all the talk of destiny and my own fervent hope, absolutely nothing came.

Except a kind of creepy, happy growl.

Bea's dad, the high priest, shook his head. I could see him glancing back at me. He motioned for me to come and take his place in the outer circle. I looked at Diane for guidance. Diane pursed her lips, and then glanced out at the woods where a kind of chortling snort could be heard. "They'll attack us without a proper circle, child. I'm sorry."

It was the "you failed" moment I'd been expecting.

"No!" Mom shouted. "Give her another chance."

"Mom," I said as I started toward the spot Bea's dad had held in the outer circle. "It's okay."

"No. No! This must be done tonight. Look at them, Diane! They've come for her, and you're giving her to them."

The song began to falter as the other coveners strained to follow the argument.

I paused. What did Mom mean? Who or what were those things in the woods? And why did they come tonight? Did it really have something to do with me? Could these be the enemies my dad talked about? Or were they on his side?

"No time to argue. They'll attack soon," Bea's dad said. He broke out of his spot in the circle. As he rushed past me, he all but shoved me into position. "Hold the line," he yelled authoritatively. "*I'm* drawing the east now."

"No, wait." It was Mom again. "You can't do this to her! What about the candles? Wasn't that wind magic? She needs a second chance!"

"We don't have time. Anyway, he has every right. He's the high priest. It's his call and I happen to agree with it," Diane said.

"No," Mom started up the argument again, but Bea's dad had already begun. I could sense the swirl of the wind tug at my hair and I heard the rattling of the leaves. I quickly grasped the waiting hands and joined the outer circle.

The creatures in the woods quieted at the show of magic.

But one stepped forward, right in front of me.

It was hard to distinguish all the details in the darkness, but it—no, he—was definitely human, and, uh, quite naked. Dappled moonlight revealed a tall, lean, muscular form with pale, almost luminescent skin. Dark hair framed a hauntingly handsome face and yellow, catlike eyes.

Looking me directly in the face, he put a hand to his heart and bowed slightly. "Princess Anastasija," he said. "My lady."

The eyes caught mine and trapped them in his gaze. Unearthly as they were, I found myself wanting to lose myself in their golden pools. A calm swept over me, and I felt a sense of homecoming. What was this wonderful, enchanting being? And why shouldn't I run wild and free into the woods with him— where I belonged?

Just as I was ready to break from the circle and take the creature by the hand, Bea's dad spoke his own words of power. The coven repeated, "So mote it be," and the wind pushed the handsome stranger back a step. He lifted an arm to ward it off, but stumbled into the shadows of the trees and disappeared completely from view.

"Wait," I implored.

But the woman holding my hand squeezed it tightly and shook her head as if to say, "No, this is best."

Although I couldn't see any movement, I could feel the others retreating as well. Their presence faded as the magic swelled.

Bea was speaking now, conjuring fire. A warm pulse filled the circle, like a sudden flare from a bonfire. The other witches sensed their departure as well, and one by one, they turned and faced the inner circle again. I was the last to turn, still hoping to see a final glimpse of the alluring otherworldly creature who called me *his* lady.

Nikolai's water was like a soft mist, and by the time Shannon solidified the circle with earth, there was no trace of the haunting presence in the woods. The coven now stood, in fact, somewhere else, a place between the real and the magical worlds.

I watched the ritual as an outsider. I saw Diane bestow the gift of prophecy on her niece, Bea. Nikolai would be a shaman, and Shannon a bard. The last bit brought a tiny tear to my eye, but I was outside them all now. This would be the last Inner Circle ritual I'd ever witness.

It all seemed removed somehow, like I'd had a heavy dose of cold medicine and my brain had gone all foggy and distant. I followed along as the four elements were thanked and released, the ritual unwinding to a close.

When the circle opened with the familiar words, "The circle is open, but unbroken. Merry meet, merry part, and merry meet again," I breathed a small sigh of relief. It hadn't been nearly as horrible as I expected. Thanks to the weird people in the woods, everyone was more focused on repelling them than on my failure.

Well, everyone except Mom.

Someone relit the circle of candles. People were crowding around Bea, Nikolai, and Shannon to congratulate them on their successful Initiation. Not moving from my spot near the circle's edge, I accepted the bug spray Grandmother Storm offered, along with the soft, understanding smile and gentle pat on the shoulder. After dosing myself with the spray, I passed it on to the next covener, who also gave me that sad, pitying look.

I didn't really want sympathy. I wanted answers. Turning, I stared out into the woods. The large, gnarled oaks stood tall and mute. Who had been out there? What were they? Had one of them really spoken to me, called me "my lady"?

Someone put an arm gently across my shoulders. I expected

to see Mom, but it was Bea's dad. "I'm sorry," he said, pushing his glasses up on his nose with his finger. "I didn't mean to be so abrupt. I thought they might attack. They seemed determined, don't you think? Much worse than before. We've got to rein them in. They're our responsibility, you know."

"Who are they?"

Bea's dad looked shocked. "Why, they're your father's people. . . ." He paused and watched my face intently in the candlelight. "Hasn't your mother ever told you?"

Dad's people? Did he mean Ramses? Was I one of whatever those things were in the woods? How was that even possible? Were they even entirely human?

Watching the expression on my face, Bea's dad paled. He removed his arm and awkwardly stepped away. "Oh. I shouldn't have said anything. You don't know about them, do you?"

"No, Mom's never said a word," I admitted. "Please tell me about them. What are they?"

"I've already said too much," Bea's dad said, anger creeping into his voice. "Your mother has been very irresponsible. You should have known about this before tonight of all nights."

I couldn't agree more. Speaking of my mother, I was about to confront her about all of this when I heard Mom's voice shrilly rising above all the happy chatter. "You will allow it. I demand a second chance for Ana."

Mom was up in Diane's face, her own red and blotchy with rage.

"You saw them," Mom continued. Voices hushed as everyone's attention shifted. "They came for her. Are you just going to let her slip into their grasp? I won't allow it. She is my daughter. Not theirs!"

As fascinated by this conversation as I was, I felt myself wanting to shrink into the dark shadows of the forest just like the others had—especially when everyone turned to look at me.

"She has none of our magic," Diane said with surprising calm. "There's nothing more to be done, Amelia. The coven will continue to protect her, but she can't be in the Inner Circle."

"No, no," Mom began her usual denial. "You saw the candles go out. That was definitely wind."

But it hadn't come from me, I thought silently.

Mom continued. "Something went wrong tonight. They were waiting. It was some kind of ambush. Maybe their presence affected her abilities. You know she has potential."

"No, I don't," I found myself screaming, despite the embarrassment. "Just stop! I can't do it. I never could. I told you that a hundred times, but you wouldn't listen."

Mom's eyes were wild with rage when she swung around to look at me. Everyone in the coven was absolutely silent, riveted to the argument. "Listen to me, young lady. This is very important. You must complete the Initiation. It is essential to your survival. You don't want to be one of them, do you?"

What was so wrong with them, anyway? "I don't know, maybe I do," I said impulsively.

A shock wave rippled through the coven.

"She doesn't know what she's saying," Mom said. Then to me, her voice quivering with anger, "You don't know what that means."

"That's because you never told her," Bea's dad's voice cut across the circle. "Amelia, you did your daughter a huge disservice. She doesn't even know what she is."

The coven exploded in a fury of "What? How can that be?"

Mom looked ready to cry. She took a few hesitating steps toward me, her arms outstretched. "Honey, I couldn't. It's . . . You don't have to be like them. You just have to find the magic inside you. I know it's there."

Mom started sobbing, because we both—no, everyone—knew the truth. If I had magic, it wasn't this kind.

"You should tell her," Bea's dad insisted.

"I can't," Mom whispered.

"Then I will," he said, and, before Mom could protest, added, "Anastasija Parker, you're a dhampyr. You're half vampire."

~~ Eight

Vampire? Okay, I was kind of almost ready for that, what with all the inferences Mom tossed around earlier with Ramses, but . . . half vampire? Really?

Vampires were real?

If I was a vampire, a half one, then that begged the question, was that what those things in the woods were—vampires? Well, if that was the case, then they were very different from what I would have expected from the movies. And, what? Now I was the princess of the vampires?

How weird was that?

Apparently everyone else in the coven must have been thinking the same thing, because they all stared, openmouthed, at me. Well, except Mom. She turned and fled from the circle in a burst of tears.

Nice. Thanks for the support, Mom.

Bea's dad no longer met my eye. Actually, when I scanned the crowd for friendly faces, most people turned away or feigned a sudden interest in the grass, their fingernails, or anything else.

I looked at Bea imploringly, hoping for a show of support from my very best and oldest friend. But instead, Bea looked back at me with barely contained horror.

Okay, now *this* was about as horrible as I imagined the Initiation was going to go. Not only did I not pass my magical test, but now I was also apparently some kind of big fat half freak.

Great.

Maybe Mom had the best exit strategy after all. Time to flee.

So I took off into the woods. I ran. I didn't care where my feet took me as long as it was "away." As I dashed through the brush, I let myself cry. Tears streamed down my cheeks, blurring my vision—which was probably how I ended up tripping on the exposed tree root and falling flat on my face into a tall stand of ostrich ferns.

I decided not to get up.

I thought maybe I might lie here forever.

Rolling over, I panted and sobbed. The ferns were soft and slick on my back. Mosquitoes hummed in the otherwise quiet, dark forest. As I stared up at the round moon, I tried to make everything add up.

Given the way the creatures—it was hard for me to think of them as vampires yet—shied away when the coven started using magic, perhaps it was no wonder I sucked at it. It was this "blood" that everyone said would "out."

Ramses had said I had another destiny, even warned me not to come tonight. Had he been attacked by this same group of vampires— What did you call a group of vampires, anyway? A "murder," like with crows? Given their feline eyes, I thought "pride" might be more accurate.

But Ramses didn't have eyes like that, did he? Of course, he was wearing clothes too. Maybe he was some different tribe or clan or "pride" or whatever.

It was all so confusing.

And I had no one to ask. The coven had abandoned me. My mom ran off. My best friend . . .

Okay, I'd kind of been prepared for the idea that when I failed the Wiccaning, the coven would freak and Mom would cry. I'd even entertained the idea that Bea might have trouble at first. I thought, with her mom and everything, she'd be the first to sympathize. But she wouldn't even meet my eye. She wouldn't even look at me.

I suppose that was better than some of the disgusted looks the other coveners shot me. At least she hadn't gaped at me in abject horror.

I groaned.

"So you yet live, my lady."

I sat up with a start. I looked around frantically for the source of the voice and found him lounging in the crook of a solitary crab apple tree. It was the one who had spoken to me before. He looked strangely natural, sitting there, like he was just another part of the wildness of the woods, like a squirrel. No, that was the wrong image. There was nothing cute or skittery about him. He was feral, yes, but more like a mountain lion, full of grace and a languid sort of danger.

He jumped down from the branches with ease. Crouching, he peered at me as though inspecting something. "You've left the circle. Were you cast out?"

I didn't think so. I'd failed, but as far as I knew, I wasn't banished or anything serious like that. No, in fact, Diane had said something about the coven still protecting me. "I'm not sure," I said honestly. "But, in a way, I am. I'm not going to be in the Inner Circle anytime soon."

He laughed slightly. "Their loss."

I wasn't sure what to make of that. Was he being sarcastic or sympathetic? After all, if Mom was right, the vampires wanted me to fail tonight. But he didn't seem all that evil. In fact, other than being naked and the funky, reflective eyes, he seemed really quite normal.

"Who are you?" I asked, and I really wanted to add, "And where *are* your clothes?" but I thought better of that last part. It seemed a bit rude, although it was really difficult to concentrate on the conversation at hand. The shadows mostly hid the salient bits from view, but I was very aware of just how close I sat to a completely naked man.

He touched his heart slightly again, in that oddly courtly gesture. "Elias Constantine, at your service."

"Are you really a vampire, Elias?" I liked the way his name felt on my tongue; it was exotic and foreign, but old-fashioned and archaic in a knightly sort of way. Not unlike my name, really.

He flinched at my choice of words, as though I'd slurred him with the term "vampire." "I've been called that," he said.

"Oh." I hadn't meant to insult him. "Well, what would you call yourself?"

He smiled slightly. "Elias, knight of the dark realm, but that's not the answer you're looking for, I know." Elias seemed to consider his answer further, his cat eyes reflecting moonlight. " 'Humanity's end,' 'Witches' Bane,' you tell me. What's your preference, my lady?"

Humanity's end? WTF? I was beginning to think "vampire"

sounded like a much nicer option. "What I mean is . . . ?" What did I ask here? His race? His species? "Um, what are you? What I really want to know is, what am I?"

In the moonlight, his smile was soft and strangely understanding. "You are your father's daughter and a very, very special lady. You are someone I am sworn to protect, and will, at the cost of my very life."

The idea that someone had pledged his life to protect me was very romantic, like something straight out of a fairy tale. Who was this guy, really?

And could he be for real?

"So you have a life? You're not, like, undead."

He laughed. "No. Not yet, anyway."

That was an interesting answer. It seemed to imply that he might become undead under certain circumstances. I left that thought for now, however. "Do you drink blood?" I asked.

Elias's amused smile faded quickly. "Yes."

Suddenly, the woods seemed very cold and deep.

He shook his head, as though he sensed my change in attitude. "The hunt is a very sacred thing, my lady. But nothing to be afraid of."

I wasn't so sure about that. I pulled my knees up under my chin, putting a bit more distance between us.

He watched with sad eyes, but didn't move from his strangely relaxed yet ready-to-pounce crouch. "Ah, my lady. Much of what you have heard about us are lies."

That was the thing, though. I hadn't heard much of anything. Tonight was the first time I'd even heard the word "vampire" outside of books and movies, much less to find out that I was half one. "Will you tell me the truth?" I asked.

Another courtly inclination of his head, and he said, "Anything you wish."

I considered what I might like to know the most. "Am I . . . are you . . . human?"

In the darkness, his expression was hard to read, especially since I kept finding myself being drawn to the way his short hair was black enough to seem almost a part of the night. His head was tipped downward as he considered my question. When I dared to look at the rest of him, I marveled at the smooth hardness of his marble white skin.

"Are we human?" he repeated. As he spoke, those cat-slit eyes caught my gaze intensely. "You seem quite desperate for that answer to be yes. Why? I wonder."

My mouth opened, though I wasn't sure what to say. Before I could formulate a response, he began again.

"You say you're still part of the coven, but where are your friends who were so intent on protecting you earlier? It took very little for them to turn on you, didn't it?" He paused, watching me. But what could I say? He was right. He nodded as though he heard my thoughts or perhaps saw my answer in my eyes. "Trust me, this is a very ancient, ingrained character trait of your adopted people, and it shows little sign of improving over time."

I frowned, feeling the sting of his remarks and a little insulted as well. I mean, I was at least half human, wasn't I? "You said you'd answer honestly, but you haven't answered my question at all."

He dipped his head as though in acquiescence, but his tone held something else entirely. "I haven't. But neither have I lied to you, my lady."

"That's a technicality," I said. It was hard to resist the urge to poke him with the toe of my shoe, because there was something about Elias that seemed open to teasing. I had to remind myself I didn't know this guy at all, and it was possible he could be quite dangerous.

Despite the threat of the sharp canines, I sensed a mischievous twinkle in the smile that spread across Elias's face. "It's a hard habit to break, this desire to misdirect. I spent centuries doing only precisely as I was told, nothing more."

"And you're still doing it." I laughed. This time I couldn't hold back the urge and nudged him playfully. "Answer the question, Elias. Are you human?"

He startled when I mentioned his name, almost as if instead of giving him a gentle poke, I'd slapped him in the face. Straightening, his eyes narrowed. His words, when they came, were very precise and clipped. "I am not. Nor have I ever been. Not the way you seem to be asking, at any rate."

Not human. I shivered, withdrawing deeper into myself. Not human.

"Now grant me a question of my own, my lady. Is it better to serve in heaven or rule in hell?"

Confused, I looked up to ask him what he meant, when suddenly I heard a shout in the distance.

"Get away from her, demon!"

The coven had found us. I could hear footfalls crashing through the underbrush. People were shouting. Magic was revving up; I felt it like static electricity building in the air. I stood up to ward them off, to tell them that it was okay, that Elias and I were just talking—

But he was already gone.

f it was possible, Mom was even angrier. Apparently, it was one thing to fail miserably as a witch, but another thing entirely to talk to a vampire in the forest *alone*.

"... irresponsible! I can't believe you talked to him when you know nothing about who they are, and what they are capable of!"

I tuned out most of Mom's argument, but I couldn't ignore this. "Oh yeah? And whose fault is that?"

Mom's lips pursed like they always did when she was mad and didn't want to say anything.

We had gone back to the cabin. A potluck meal had been laid out, but almost no one was eating. The large, open room smelled of five-bean casserole and roasting peppers.

People collected in small, subdued knots of conversation near the food tables. Mom had corralled me on the opposite side of the room and had been berating me in harsh whispers. Every so often, eyes strayed in our direction, people trying to eavesdrop subtly.

I'd mostly shut down. I hated being the center of attention even when it was something cool, like my birthday. Now everyone was staring at me like something you might find on the bottom of your shoe.

I'd failed the test. I'd expected that. But I came here not knowing why, thinking I was just some big witch-fail. Now from what I could tell, the way magic reacted to me might not entirely be my fault. I was half vampire. Didn't that have something to do with it? Shouldn't Mom have warned me? "I told you that I couldn't do magic," I said. "Didn't it ever occur to you that maybe that was because I was a damp . . . a whatever, a half vampire?"

"Dhampyr," Mom said quietly. She'd been twisting her lips and staring at the floor, but now she looked me in the eye. "Yes, it occurred to me."

"Why didn't you tell me? I mean, you knew I was going to fail."

"No, I didn't," Mom insisted with a sniff. "You might have passed. You are half human and Parker blood is strong."

"Not strong enough," I said.

Mom put her hand on my shoulder kindly. "You have the gift. I've felt it in you. If they'd only give you another chance, I'm sure—"

I shrugged out from under Mom's touch. How many times did I have to explain all this? I was a failure, plain and simple.

"I know you can feel magic," Mom said. "You're not entirely lost to me."

I had been starting to walk away, ostensibly to get something from the potluck tables. I wasn't hungry, but I didn't want to talk about any of this anymore. Mom's words stopped me. It was true. How had Mom known?

When I turned back to look, Mom was nodding her head. "See. This is why I never gave up on you. I know you're a witch, not one of them."

Them! Ugh! Mom made it sound like that nice, albeit naked, guy in the woods was some kind of monster. I hated how horrified Mom sounded. With a shake of my head, I turned my back on Mom. I slid the door open and headed outside. If only I had my license! Then I could hop in the car and drive home, just get out of here.

At this rate, I'd be thirty before I got my driver's license. I could hardly stand to be in the same room as Mom. How could we ever get enough time together behind the wheel for me to qualify?

Crap. As if there hadn't been enough fallout already.

I walked through the sea of parked cars and started down the road. I had to get out of here and I couldn't stand to drive home with Mom. My thought was to walk to the main road and see if there was some kind of public transportation. This was some crazy way-outer-ring suburb, and I knew most buses in the Cities stopped only at the first-tier suburbs. Still, maybe I could hitch. Heck, I was half vampire—perhaps I could sprout bat wings and fly home!

Silently, Nikolai appeared at my side.

"Hey," he said, startling me out of my reverie.

"Jeez, you scared the crap out of me," I said, after catching my breath. "Where'd you come from?"

"You shouldn't be out here alone," he admonished. "You never know what might come out of the woods."

"Oh, you mean like you?"

"Ha," he said, but his smile had just enough of a trace of mischievousness to give me pause. "No, I meant like our visitors."

"The vampires."

Nikolai put a finger to his lips. "Don't say their name, especially *that* one. Their hearing is incredible."

I halted my insistent march toward the road. "You sound like you know things about them."

"Are you kidding? My people have been hunters for centuries."

"Vampire hunters? You mean like Buffy?"

Nikolai shook his head. "We can't talk about this out in the open. I came out here to make sure you were okay. Let's get back inside."

To the awkward? No way. I knew Nikolai had his own car and a license, and, it seemed, he also had a lot of information about *my* people. "I can't deal with my mom right now. Would you give me a ride home?"

He smiled as if he'd wanted to offer all along. "Sure."

I used my cell to leave a message on the landline at home. That way, once Mom had cooled down and wondered where I'd gotten to, she wouldn't have to worry. Not that it probably mattered, given that Mom considered me one of "them" now.

Nikolai showed the way to a decrepit Toyota. I thought it might have been green under all the rust and duct tape. The engine made an ominous sound when it started up. The radio blared a heavy metal station, which Nikolai quickly switched off. I felt a little self-conscious as I put on my seat belt.

I'd never really been alone with Nikolai before. Bea would be so jealous! But I could feel a serious case of nerves building. I didn't know how to act or what to do. Should I compliment him on the retro cool pink furry dice hanging from the rearview? What were you supposed to say to a guy when you first got into his car? The worst part was Bea would know. Of course, she wasn't here, and it wasn't even entirely clear if we were still friends.

"Hey, I got you a present," Nikolai said, rummaging through the backseat while the car idled noisily. The interior smelled of patchouli and old fast food. Nikolai kept the floorboards in the front pretty neat, but the backseat was strewn with schoolbooks, papers, and empty pop cans. From somewhere in the chaos, he unearthed a thin, brightly wrapped package. Flicking on the overhead dome light, he said, "Here!"

I took the pretty, light gift with a shy smile. "You didn't have to get me anything. You really shouldn't have."

"Come on, it's your birthday. Of course I did."

Nikolai or someone had wrapped the gift professionally. Cartoonish, brightly colored dancing kittens decorated the paper. Thin pink and yellow ribbon had been curled into festive bows.

"Open it up," he insisted.

I carefully found the tape and undid the edges.

He sighed dramatically. "Aw, rip into it, would you?"

With a smile, I pulled the paper until it shredded in my hands. Not sure what to do with the paper, I handed it to Nikolai, who tossed it into the back.

Finally, a CD case was revealed. I inspected the label. Horrified, I discovered it wasn't a band I recognized. I felt mortified that I couldn't express genuine enthusiasm. The more seconds passed, the deeper I was aware of my social faux pas. "Um," I finally said, alternately trying to see his reaction and avoiding making eye contact. "Thanks! I'm sure I'll like it. I just . . . um. Who is this?"

He laughed. "You know, most girls would have just completely faked it. I love that you're honest. Not like the rest of them," he said somewhat wistfully, and trailed off as if lost in thought. After a shake of his head as though to clear it, he tapped a finger on the CD case. "This is my band. It's not a hundred percent professional or anything, but we rented a real recording studio. Most of our stuff is MP3s that we're selling online, but I burned them all on here and made up liner notes and cover art for you."

My eyes widened. "That is so cool." I looked more closely at the CD. Sure enough, there was Nik standing among a group of guys all decked out in leather on the cover, looking really . . . sexy. "This is you? Wow."

"Well, wait until you hear it. And then, if you like it, maybe you could post a review? That'd be awesome."

I agreed, although why anyone would care what I thought I didn't know. Maybe I could make a niche on the Web as the half-vampire chick and be really big with "other siders" or Witches' Bane or whatever they called themselves.

"It's a really nice gift," I said, looking around for somewhere to put it. I didn't carry a purse and it was too big to fit in the back pocket of my jeans. Besides, I didn't think sitting on it was a good idea. I might have slipped it into a front pocket of one of those oversized shirts I usually wore, but instead I was wearing a very skin-hugging halter top and a blouse without pockets. Looking down at my own décolletage suddenly, I felt another blush brewing. Especially since when I looked up, I saw that Nikolai was looking there too.

"That's a beautiful necklace," he told my chest. Reaching out a finger, he looped it around one strand and slid the goddess pendant out from her hiding spot between my breasts.

I think he pulled my breath right out of my chest too.

"It has a lot of power," he said, caressing one of the stones in his fingers. As he leaned closer to examine it, his long hair nearly brushed my skin. I could smell his shampoo, clean and spicy. "Did you make it?"

When he looked up, his eyes were right next to mine. We could have kissed, except I was completely flummoxed. "Uh, no," I managed to say. "Bea did."

"She's quite the artist," he said, letting the necklace drop. He didn't immediately move away, and I noticed the stubble on his chin and how his eyes held the fiery color of liquid amber.

I started to reach a hand up to touch his face, but stopped myself in time. "Your eyes . . . I've never seen a color like that."

He looked away, as if embarrassed. "It runs in the family—Algerian, I guess."

"Oh, well, they're beautiful." Beautiful? Did you say that to a boy? "I mean, handsome."

"Do you get tired of people noticing your eyes?" he asked. His gaze searched mine for a moment; then he looked away and muttered something I almost didn't hear, but which sounded like, "And talking about your stupid destiny?"

I touched his arm so he'd turn and look at me again. "Yes. My mom never shuts up about it."

He nodded. "Kirov boys are always hunters."

"Parker girls always pass their Initiation."

We shared a smile and a kind of sad laugh, and then he said,

"Sucks about the Initiation." I had nothing to say to that, but luckily, he added, "Anyway, I hope you like the music."

"Oh, um, yeah." Heat flooded my body. I felt like we were standing on the edge of something deep and real, but I didn't know how to take the next step.

"Uh," I said, groping. "I can't wait to listen to the CD. Are you the lead singer?" I thought I saw his nod, but I continued babbling nervously. "That's just so awesome. I don't know anyone who has a CD. Did you write your own music? Wow. But, uh, we should probably get going. I've got school tomorrow. I totally flunked a precalculus test today, so I should really study. I mean, not that I really want to, but, you know. . . ."

God, I felt stupid. How idiotic must I sound right now? He probably thought I was a complete dork. I sucked at being a witch *and* I sucked at talking to boys. Wow, what a capper for an all-round suck-ass birthday.

Somehow getting the hint, Nikolai turned off the dome light. "Tonight was kind of weird, huh?" he said, as he switched on the headlights and adjusted the mirrors.

I laughed, relieved at the darkness and the change of subject. My total botch-up tonight wasn't my favorite thing to talk about, but at least it was more familiar ground. I shrugged off his concern. "Don't feel bad. I knew it was going to happen." When he gave me a curious look, I added, "Seriously. I haven't been able to do magic, like, ever."

"No, I meant with the vampires. I've never seen so many of them. Up close."

"Oh."

Nikolai nudged the car out onto the long, narrow path.

To crack the window, I had to use a manual crank handle. As

I struggled with the clumsy contraption, I wondered what his vampire-hunting family would think about him giving me a ride home. I bet there were rules about hunter/vampire interactions.

But I was only half, so did that count? I still couldn't quite wrap my head around it all. I didn't even really know what it meant to be a vampire. "So your family hunts vampires? What's that like?"

"We don't really do it much here. But my dad was big into it, mostly when he was in Russia. Eastern Europe has a lot more of them. Romania is riddled, really."

"Yeah?" Why hadn't I ever heard of this? You'd think it would make national news: a vampire plague in Romania.

But Nikolai just nodded like it *was* common knowledge. "Yeah."

His last noncommittal words hung in the air between us, and Nikolai seemed to be studying my face now. I didn't know what kind of reaction he was expecting. Was I supposed to be mad that his dad presumably killed a bunch of Romanian vampires? It wasn't like I had any friends who were vampires. Well, okay, I knew Elias and Ramses, but none of us had exchanged more than a few words. I glanced out into the night. Was Ramses okay? Had Elias evaded the coven?

My heart thudded dully at that last thought. What would they do with him if they did catch him?

"Your dad . . . he hunts for the coven now, I bet," I said. What had Bea's dad said? Something about how the vampires were their responsibility? More mysteries. I was beginning to feel like every new bit of information came with its own set of questions.

"Yep, he does," Nikolai said. Again his tone betrayed no

emotion and he watched me almost as carefully as he did the road. "I'm his apprentice. My damn destiny."

This was the second time Nikolai made it sound like he wasn't too excited about being a vampire hunter. Was I supposed to bond with him about that? What if he was testing me, trying to figure out which side I would ultimately fall on?

Thing is, I didn't really know. The vampires I'd met all seemed completely undeserving of the reaction they got. Ramses hadn't done anything to provoke the cocoon-from-hell spell. Elias seemed so . . . naked, but not, well, otherwise dangerous. Meanwhile, my supposed friends all got super judgmental and cruel when it came to vampires.

I wanted to be direct since Nikolai seemed to appreciate that, but something warned me off that approach this time. Instead, I asked, "The vampires—they're not human. Are they hard to kill?"

After watching for traffic, we turned out onto the county highway. "Well, they hate our magic. They can't fight it, unless they're willing to spill blood. Their own." He gave me a sidelong look, and I wasn't sure what it meant. "At least that's what my dad says. He's the guy you should really talk to, and believe me: he loves to go on about the good old days in Russia and the Great Uprising."

Somehow I knew we weren't talking about anything I'd read in my history books. "What was that?"

"Honestly, I tune a lot of it out," he admitted with a sheepish grin. "But somehow the vampires figured out that they had their own kind of magic, blood magic, which would counter our own. A long-ago vampire king sacrificed himself to a hunt and broke the spell of binding our ancestors used to keep them at bay."

"Wow." I was sure I wasn't supposed to, but I found myself thinking how noble that vampire king had been.

Nikolai didn't seem to notice, however. "The binding spell still remains in all of them. So when we hunt, we tap that spell, and then plunge a magical dagger in their heart."

When he mimed stabbing, I jumped a little.

"Don't worry. You might not be a True Witch," Nikolai said, "but unless the Elders say otherwise, you're still in the coven. We don't go after our own, no matter what."

Well, there was a comforting thought. At least I didn't have to worry about being stabbed by Nikolai's dad in my sleep. For now, at least, as Nik so clearly implied. How much longer until we reached the city? I suddenly felt really vulnerable out in the open of the cornfields and prairie.

At least I did until I saw the flash of white out of the corner of my eye. Something was pacing us. No deer could run that fast. But I pretended not to see it, and even though I wasn't entirely certain it *was* a vampire, I secretly smiled. Elias had said he would protect me. Maybe he really meant it.

I didn't want Nikolai to notice, though. Quickly, I distracted him. "It's kind of obvious that I don't know anything about vampires. What's the big deal, anyway? I mean, my mom, uh, dated one. They can't be that bad, can they?"

Even in the dark I could see Nikolai's arched eyebrow and hardening look. This was the sympathy I wasn't supposed to show, I could tell. His voice was cold as ice. "They're blood-suckers, Ana. They are the enemy I've trained my entire life to defeat."

I ignored the threat in his voice and tried to sound breezy and light when I asked, "So they kill people for food?"

Nikolai didn't have a ready answer for that, at least. His fierce mask crumbled a little as he fumbled for the words. "Well, not exactly. If you ask them, they babble on about a mystical hunt or something, but my dad says they're predators who will even kill their own."

I was glad Nikolai couldn't see my face pale.

He seemed to be inspecting me again anyway. "I don't even know how we let it happen. I mean, if it's true, what they said, that you're half vampire."

I didn't much like the look he was giving me and, moreover, I didn't know what to say. After all, I had no idea how Mom and Ramses ever got together either, especially considering how Mom reacted to Ramses today. So I looked out the window at the corn and alfalfa fields passing by at sixty miles an hour, hoping to see another glimpse of my other-earthly protector.

I started when Nikolai put a hand on my knee. His palm was warm, but firm. It seemed gentle, imploring, and full of concern. But he pulled it back quickly. So fast, in fact, that I didn't get a chance to say that I sort of liked his touch; I'd just been surprised.

"Hey," Nikolai said. "I'm sorry. I didn't mean to insult you. It's just hard to imagine a vampire and a person, you know, together. It's sort of like hearing that a lion and an antelope had a baby."

"Nice analogy," I sneered sarcastically. "I don't feel insulted at all."

"I should probably stop talking," he admitted sheepishly with a little laugh. "Open mouth. Insert foot."

He seemed honestly embarrassed, and it wasn't like I couldn't get where he was coming from. Like he'd said, all his life he'd been trained to destroy vampires. It must be hard for him to imagine making love, not war, as it were.

A flush heated my face as the image passed through my brain. I glanced at Nikolai shyly from under my lashes. It was so confusing how I felt about him. He was awfully good-looking and clearly into me, but he made me nervous too.

"Don't stop talking," I begged. "It's nice to finally get some information. Even if I don't really like what I hear."

"I suppose that's why your mom never said much. She didn't want to hurt your feelings."

"I suppose," I agreed, but I wasn't entirely convinced. I figured Mom was just embarrassed about her past. Or completely hated Ramses and would rather not even think about him. Anyway, I didn't really want to talk about Mom. My mind, instead, remembered the way Elias moved so freely through the trees. "Do they have some kind of kinship with nature or something? Vampires, I mean. And why no clothes? I always thought they'd be into tuxes and stuff."

The onslaught of questions apparently made Nikolai laugh. "One at a time," he said with a chuckle. "Vampires hunt naked, like animals. It's part of the ritual. Some people say they do that because they can transform into wolves, but I don't buy it. It violates the law of conservation of mass."

"True enough," I said. "Plus that would be magic and they can't do magic."

"Mostly," Nikolai agreed. He slowed down to stop at one of those lonely stop signs on the prairie where you could see the empty traffic lanes going on for miles in all directions.

Mostly? I considered that and then said, "There's the blood magic. Plus, they seem awfully comfortable in the woods. They must be okay with nature magic."

I thought about my own skill in the garden. Was that from my dad's side, as it were?

"I don't really know," Nikolai said with a shrug. "Most of my experience is theoretical, you know. Tonight was the first time I'd seen one—more than one—so close."

We accelerated back up to speed as Nikolai manually shifted gears, the engine gunning like a race car the whole time. We'd gotten to the US highway, and things quickly started to feel like city again. Nikolai's car merged into a stream of vehicles. Billboards bathed in harsh electric light rose up over rooftops and noise barriers.

"They're a little spooky," I admitted, thinking of the way they'd circled us and laughed like a pack of ravenous hyenas.

"The entire coven was totally freaked. I thought we were going to die."

"Do they hate witches or something?"

Nikolai glanced at me. "Just a little," he said, but his tone was sarcastic.

Well, if Mom's reaction to Ramses was any indication, the feeling was mutual. It seemed a bit more than some kind of long-standing feud, like the Montagues and Capulets of *Romeo and Juliet*. So much for the hope that Mom and Ramses were romantic star-crossed lovers.

"You're thinking pretty hard about something," Nik said. "It's funny. Everyone thinks you're so quiet, but I can tell—you've just got a lot going on inside. It's something I've always liked about you."

Was that a compliment? Did he just call me smart? Was smart

sexy? And "always"? Did that mean he'd noticed me before to-night? "Uh. I guess."

"No, no, it's a good thing. Trust me," Nikolai said, his eyes flicking between me and the now heavy traffic. "You don't just say whatever comes into your head like some girls. And you don't waste a lot of time with small, meaningless talk. When you finally make up your mind to speak, it's usually something different and interesting."

Now he was calling me weird? But he liked it?

"Like with my tattoo, everybody always asks, 'Did it hurt?' like, what, they thought I went to some brand-new pain-free artist? I mean, how dumb are most people?"

Yet it was one of the first things I'd said. "But it looks so raw, it only makes sense people would ask."

He shook his head. "You're being too kind. It's not that they say, 'It looks like it still hurts,' like you did. They just say whatever dumb crap flies through their head. No thought at all to how it might come off."

I hadn't really considered all that, but I was just as happy to be done with vampires for the time being. Minneapolis's downtown skyline rose in front of us, a collection of tightly grouped skyscrapers and several smaller, beautiful churches. The basilica, in particular, always impressed me with its carved white marble walls and copper-domed roof, green with oxidation, illuminated in the bright spotlight.

When I looked back, Nikolai was smiling. "You know what else I like about you?"

I was afraid to ask, since so far he seemed to appreciate my dorkiness, not one of my usual top-ten awesome things about myself.

"You're not afraid of silence. So many girls just chatter to fill the void. Like your friend Beatrice. Does she ever stop talking to think?"

"That's not fair," I said quickly in defense of my best friend. "Bea is very outgoing. She's very smart about people and funny too. I think she likes you, you know."

The highway curved and pretty soon the bulk of downtown was in the rearview.

"I know," Nikolai said with a snort of disgust. "It's pretty obvious. Not a subtle bone in her body, is there?"

Well, it was one of Bea's shortcomings, I had to admit. "No, not really."

"I was wondering," Nikolai said, sneaking another glance at me. "You want to get coffee sometime or something?"

Oh God. He was asking me out on a date.

Ten

As my heart pounded clean out of my chest, he continued. "It's just that a couple of friends of mine like to go bowling at this really funky alley. I think you'd appreciate it. It's quirky, but a lot of fun. You get these goofy shoes, and•the whole place smells of popcorn and alley grease. Anyway, I'd love to take you. You know, if you want to come sometime?"

Bowling with his friends? That actually sounded kind of cool. "Yeah, I'd like that," I agreed.

"Great. So, can I call you?"

"Of course. Uh, where's your phone?"

He pointed to the cup holder that held his cell. I opened it up and, after a few seconds, figured out how to save my number in his directory. It was kind of a big step. I'd never given my number to a boy before.

Oh, what was Bea going to say? I'd just totally stolen Bea's boyfriend, even if he clearly didn't think he was. As if she didn't have enough reasons to hate me right now.

We crossed the Mississippi River, a ribbon of darkness in the electric glimmer of the city, and soon Nikolai had exited on Dale and headed into my neighborhood. Thanks to Mom's superpowered wards, we actually drove past my own house. Twice.

"That's weird," Nikolai said, peering up at the darkened Victorian, as I unbuckled myself. "What's up with the cloaking device?"

"Dad, remember? Mom freaked out when he came by, and, like, disappeared us. Bea almost couldn't find us either and she's been over a million times."

"Wow," Nikolai said.

I hesitated with my hand on the door latch. I thought I should probably just go, but he had my number now and I wondered if, maybe, he might try to kiss me. Should I let him?

I looked at him hopefully for a few seconds. When he shifted slightly in his seat, I completely chickened out. I flung open the door and nearly jumped onto the sidewalk. "Thanks for the ride. I had a great time."

"Me too," he said, his elbow leaning on the steering wheel. He picked up his cell. "I'll call you about bowling, okay?"

"Yeah," I said. "I'd really like that."

I managed to say good-bye without being too much more of an idiot, and he waited at the curb like a gentleman until I turned the key in the lock and stepped inside.

Well, I thought, clutching my keys and Nik's CD to my chest in excitement. At least tonight wasn't a total loss.

IT WAS ALWAYS STRANGE COMING into the house when it was empty. Naturally dark and cavernous, it seemed doubly so at night when no one was around.

"Mom?" I called into the house, and then, just to make sure, "Dad?"

No answer from either. Since I hadn't seen Mom's car out front, I was expecting the house to be quiet, but it always paid to be certain. Quickly locking the door behind me, I kicked off my shoes next to the parson's bench. I scurried upstairs to the safety and comfort of my own room. I didn't want to be exposed when Mom came home. Who even knew what kind of mood she'd be in, but I couldn't face any more talk of vampires or Initiations. I just wanted to be normal.

To that end, I started to strip out of the clothes I'd chosen. Realizing I still had Nikolai's CD, I set it next to my laptop on my desk. Then I chucked the halter and jeans into the growing pile in the hamper in the bottom of the closet. I stood for a second in my underwear and bra trying to decide what to wear—and what Nikolai saw in me.

My figure was pathetic. You could count my ribs, and I didn't have enough on the top or the rear for my tastes. Still, Nikolai sure had found plenty to stare at. I guessed my legs were pretty nice, but . . . well, maybe some guys liked the stick-skinny thing? I did look a bit otherworldly with my ultrapale skin and mis-matched eyes.

Of course, turns out, I actually was a *vampire* princess. Jeez.

With a sigh, I shrugged into my comfiest pair of jeans and my old, tattered *Sailor Moon* T-shirt. I smiled at the cartoonish fig-ures on my chest, thinking of Taylor, remembering our obses-sion with the show way back when. I should probably try to mend fences. I needed all the friends I could get now.

Flipping open my phone, I sent Taylor a quick text, just say-ing hi. And then two seconds later another that said, "Sorry."

While I waited for a response, I went over to my desk and sat down in front of my laptop. I switched on the lamp and inspected the CD more closely. It was clear he made it just for me. Another personal gift. I felt really honored.

I looked at the picture of the band again. It was hard to believe that was Nikolai. He looked so grown-up and, uh, well, *super*hot.

Nikolai was always cute, but he'd clearly gotten all glammed up for the cover shoot, and the look he gave the camera was downright smoldering.

My phone tweedled. It was Taylor. Apparently, she was over at some friend's house gaming. The usual.

What did Taylor know about Nikolai? She knew about his band, but what about him? He'd graduated, what, last year, but I thought she might know some of the people he hung around with. Wasn't one of the guys in his band in our class? I texted a bunch of quick questions, and then set the phone down on the desktop.

I carefully removed the CD from its case and slid it into the laptop. It took only a second for the player to launch, and suddenly the room was filled with the pounding of speed-metal guitar.

Not my usual taste—I mostly went for the more funky, edgy alternative sound of Animal Collective—but I listened carefully, fascinated to hear Nikolai's singing voice.

I almost didn't hear the phone beep. I checked. It was Taylor; she did remember Nik and thought he was wicked hot. Did I know he was in a band?

I had to laugh. Hadn't she told me six times today at school? I wrote back that I was listening to his CD right now.

Through the computer speakers, Nikolai's voice resonated. It was much stronger and richer than I would have expected. He was good. I was very impressed.

Taylor sent back a "squee," and wanted to know how I'd scored a copy so soon. There was supposed to be some kind of unofficial release party at Nikolai's apartment next week. It was a house-party type thing to help promote their self-produced album. Taylor implied it was even hard to get tickets to that.

Before answering, I picked up the CD again. Nikolai was certainly a dark horse. Even though we saw each other at witchy events, he'd never mentioned all this band stuff. Maybe he didn't want to seem like he was bragging? Of course, Bea had known. Bea stuck to Nikolai's side like glue whenever he showed up at events. I tended to leave her to her flirting, and found other people to hang with when she was going all batty-eyelashes at him. I was sort of embarrassed on her behalf and, anyway, no one likes to be a third wheel.

I texted Taylor a simple question: "Will B. be jealous?"

It was hardly less than ten seconds before Taylor replied. "Oh hell, yeah."

I closed the phone with a snap. I didn't want to come between Bea and the object of her fantasies, but I was really starting to like Nikolai . . . and it wasn't my fault he asked me out, was it?

I let my head fall against the back of the chair, and I shut my eyes in frustration.

Just then there was a knock on my window.

My window? I was two stories up!

Eleven

Nervously, I glanced in the direction of the window. It was open, the screen letting in the cool evening air. Squinting to see past the light of my room into the darkened tree branches, I thought I saw a sleek figure crouching among the branches.

Vampire!

But was it Elias? Ramses?

"Anastasija?"

It had to be Ramses. No one else called me by my full first name, or with such a poetic lilt. I turned off my desk lamp and used my stocking feet to roll the chair closer to the window.

With the light off, I could see Ramses much clearer. He, thank the Goddess, wore regular clothes—well, with the exception of shoes. Apparently, vampires needed bare feet to climb trees.

Otherwise, he had on dark jeans and a plain dark blue shirt. If it was possible, he almost looked more ridiculous fully dressed sitting in the tree like some overgrown boy.

"Hey, Dad," I said with a little awkward wave. "Sorry Mom, you know, kicked your ass before. Um, are you okay?"

Over the metal song, I heard my phone ring with the receipt of another text. I ignored it for now. Besides, what would I write? "Sorry, brb, dad in tree"?

Ramses touched his side tentatively, but nodded. "Fortunately for me, my captain of the guard doesn't take orders well. It seems that I was rescued from my own stupidity by insubordination."

He seemed to think that was funny, so I smiled along like I had a clue what he was talking about. "As for the ass kicking . . ." Ramses gave a little self-deprecating chuckle. "Let's just say I really hate magic."

"Yeah, so I've heard."

I stared at the man half hidden in the long, gnarled branches of the pine tree, thinking that the butt of his jeans must be completely covered with pitch by now. Maybe that's why vampires preferred to do their tree hopping naked. Less laundry.

"I don't think we were ever *properly* introduced," he said, inclining his head as though to apologize for a breach of courtly etiquette. "I am Alexander Ramses, high prince of the dark realms and protectorate of the territories of the New World."

He seemed to be waiting for a response, so I said, "Uh, so, I'm Anastasija Ramses Parker, queen of the high school losers."

He didn't laugh at my lame joke or even crack much of a smile. I must have inherited my sense of humor from Mom. Now, there was a scary thought.

"She gave you my name, at least."

We sat in silence for a moment considering that. Then, cautiously, he added, "How'd the Initiation go?"

I snorted a laugh. "It pretty much sucked. I failed out, and then your buddies showed up and now everyone knows I'm a damp-thingy."

"Dhampyr," he corrected kindly. "It's an ugly term, half-breed. You don't have to accept it when you live among your people."

"What, in the trees? Dad, I have to go to school. I can't exactly run away to the circus. Besides, Nikolai says you're a blood-sucker. And everyone thinks you're bad juju."

Ramses listened to the barrage of insults calmly. He nodded his head as though in acknowledgment. "But what do *you* think?"

I bit my lip. Of course, I wasn't certain, but it was bizarre as heck to be chatting up a dad I never knew while he was casually sitting on a tree branch like it was a regular piece of furniture. "I think Mom will be pissed if she finds out you came to talk to me."

Conveniently, my phone buzzed again, this time with a call. The caller ID said it was Mom.

"Speak of the devil," I said as I got up to shut the window. "I have to go. That's my phone."

The window slid down before he could finish saying what sounded suspiciously like, "I love you."

Okay, now, that was something I definitely couldn't cope with right now. Love? From a vampire stranger? No. Maybe later, thank you. I turned away from the weirdness in the tree and grabbed my phone. I got it before the last ring. Of course, I had to turn down the volume on the player to hear.

I'd hardly even said hello before the shouting started. "I'm sorry," I said after the tirade had quieted. "I thought you'd check the phone here first. I left a message that I got a ride home with Nikolai."

"So you're home? Alone?"

Yeah, like I'd invite Nikolai in? What did Mom think? Or did she suspect Dad was hiding out in the tree? I switched on the light with a sigh.

"Alone," I agreed. Of course, I didn't exactly mention Ramses sitting in the branches, but, you know, it wasn't like he was in the house or anything.

"Well, I'm just turning onto Fairview now. I'll be home in ten minutes," Mom said with the strong implication that there would be more to this conversation then.

"Great," I said, trying not to sound as deeply disappointed as I was.

After we'd said our good-byes, I checked my in-box on the phone. Taylor had left a message, or, really, a big question: "R U and Nik . . . ????"

I turned up the music and thought about how to respond to Taylor's text. It was only a car ride and a conversation, after all. But he had given me his music, and I'd given him my phone number. Plus, he said he would call. But didn't older guys say that all the time? He'd asked me out . . . but bowling. With his friends. It wasn't like it was dinner and a movie, just the two of us.

"Not exactly," I wrote back, but then added, "Ask me @ school."

Maybe I'd have it figured out by then.

I MANAGED TO AVOID FURTHER conversation with Mom that night by switching off my light and pretending to already be asleep. It was a cheap cop-out, okay, but I just couldn't deal. When I didn't respond to her shouts from downstairs, Mom poked her head in the door. Through my closed eyes, I sensed her standing in the doorway for a long time, saying nothing. Finally, Mom sneaked in and gave me a light kiss on the forehead like she used to when I was a little girl.

Miraculously, not long after, I fell asleep. For real.

When I woke to the sound of my alarm beeping, I had the sensation of having dreamed about vampires and stakes and maybe even *Buffy the Vampire Slayer*, only it was Nikolai or his dad . . . or the president?

Dreams, who could figure them?

Sleepy fingers fumbled the switch of the alarm, and I rubbed my head trying to banish the last jumbled bits of the dream. I stumbled blearily out of bed. Looking down at my rumpled shirt, I realized I forgot to change into pajamas last night. Well, at least getting dressed would be easy this morning.

I gathered my schoolbooks and papers into my backpack, wondering what I was supposed to have read for history class and whether I'd have time to catch up during free period.

Despite it all, I smiled, because you know what? It was all so blessedly normal. I knocked on the wood of the doorframe as I passed through. Hopefully, things would stay that way.

Mom was in the dining room munching Cheerios and making notes in a gigantic book, *The Cosmic Mother* or some such. Her glasses were perched up on her head, almost lost in the mess of curls. I thought about escaping out the door, but the damn step creaked, and Mom caught my eye.

"Hey," she said in a tone that clearly implied come-sit-we-should-talk.

Crap.

"Hi," I replied, still eyeing the door. Could I pretend I was late? I checked my watch. Crap, I had hours before school started. I gave up with a sigh. Setting my backpack by my shoes near the door, I headed for the table. Might as well plunge right in: "Crazy night last night, huh?"

"It's going to be all right," Mom said.

I sat down in my usual spot, kitty-corner. She reached out and grasped my hand lightly. I stared at her hand. The gesture was kind of a big show of affection from Mom. "Uh, sure," I said, resisting the urge to pull away.

She released me first. "I talked to Diane and the others. They agreed we couldn't let them have you. We're going to do a rite of protection. You'll still be in the coven, as a full True Witch."

"But I can't do magic."

"Inconsequential," she insisted. "Besides, you probably can." Before I could even react to that, Mom barreled on. "I explained to them how you can feel our power. It's a manifestation of some variety; they had to admit to that. It'd be a liability in the hands of the dark kingdom."

The dark kingdom of which I was a princess, I presumed?

"The Elders want to wait until the next full moon, which I think is utter foolishness given the attack last night, but I didn't want to jeopardize the concessions I'd already won." Mom sounded so intense, and her face was so tight I thought it might shatter into tears any minute. She pulled her glasses down onto her nose and shook her head as if in answer to some unheard argument. "Stupid. Still, there's no moving those old bats once they get their minds set."

Old bats? The venerable Elders? It almost made me laugh to hear Mom so spiteful.

"And I only have so much authority," she said.

Which was also a strange thing to say, since we were supposed to be egalitarian, so technically she had no more power than anyone else.

"Well, we'll just have to keep you safe until then." Mom looked at me, as if suddenly remembering I was present for this whole rant. "I'm afraid I can't allow you out after dark anymore."

"*What?*" The force of my own angry surprise brought me to my feet. Not now, not when I had a potential date with Nikolai on the horizon. "No freaking way!"

Mom stood up and tried to grasp my hand again, but I whipped it away from her. "It's the only way, dear. I'm sorry. I have to keep you safe."

I stomped toward the door. Let her try and stop me. "You know what? Maybe I don't want to be safe!"

A magic barrier surrounded the door; I felt the buzz like pins and needles in my hand when I touched the knob. I glared at Mom. Was she really intending to hold me prisoner? "What, now I can't go to school?"

"I thought about that," she said. "But there's no need to take you out of school yet. They can't approach you during the daylight. It's only nighttime that's a problem." She had a soft, loving expression on her face, which only infuriated me more. How dare she look at me like that when she's telling me I'm under house arrest for something I didn't even do! "Honey, please," she implored. "It's only for a month."

A month! Oh my God!

But I'd never get out if I pushed her. I decided to try to play it cool. I blinked, as if shaking out my anger, and put on my best theater-schooled expression of acquiescence. "Oh, okay. If you think it's best."

That last line might have sunk it, because my ears heard unintentional sarcasm. I watched Mom's eyes, but she seemed to buy it. A relieved sigh dropped the tension from her shoulders and the magic from the door. The lock clicked open, and my arm stopped feeling prickled. "Thank you, Ana. Really, this is for the best. I'll cancel my group tonight so we can be home together, okay?"

Oh, yeah, great. "Okay," I said, trying to seem sincerely grateful.

She seemed to see through that a little. "I know it's not your favorite thing to hang out with your mom, but we can make it fun, can't we? Maybe rent one of those anime shows you like so much?" Mom pointed at my shirt hopefully.

"Sure," I said. It took all my acting skills not to gag.

She patted my shoulder, and I felt a surge of magic well up. Dark and heavy, like a gathering storm, the power tasted of metal and clinked like chains. But just as it nearly seeped into me, trapping me, the magic withdrew. "See you tonight?"

I nodded, not trusting my voice. Had Mom just considered compelling me? Was she seriously going to put a magical fetter on me to force me to obey? Unreal. There was no freaking way I was coming home tonight! I held on to my smile, however, as I picked up my backpack and let Mom open the door for me.

"See you," I lied.

Twelve

My hand shook as I handed over five dollars for a latte. The cashier gave me a curious look, but didn't ask. I scurried over to a table to wait for them to call my drink. Checking my wallet, I had about ten dollars and some change. Not a lot to run away on, but what was I going to do? The feeling had been unmistakable. Mom was about to use her magic to control me.

So she didn't actually, but she thought about it—powered up, even. That was beyond uncool. That was screwed up.

And all for what? To protect me from the scary vampires, who, as far as I could tell, just liked to sit in trees and talk. Okay, so Elias admitted they drank blood, but it was all part of some ceremonial hunt, right? Nothing evil.

Not like my mom.

Shit.

At least I had my cell phone. Even though it was forbidden at school, I'd tucked it into my pocket this morning out of habit. I stuffed it into my backpack, wondering if I was seriously considering being homeless tonight.

I was so lost in thought I almost missed my drink. Grabbing it, I headed for the bus stop. My bus picked me up on Summit, about three blocks from my house and conveniently located a half of one from the coffee shop. The morning had a nip to it, like it was intent on becoming autumn after all. I could see the steam rising from the hole in the lid of my cup, and I regretted not grabbing a coat, especially since the air smelled of rain.

I waved at the sullen skater dude who shared my stop. He always wore tattered cutoffs and had that spray-painted board leaned up against one leg. His hair was a rat's nest of product and genuine grease, but, despite the studied hoodlum look, I knew he lived in a huge mansion just up the street. His folks were probably filthy rich. I thought his name was Ted and that he might be a senior at Stassen, but we had an unspoken agreement not to converse outside of grunted hellos. Sipping my coffee, I leaned my butt against the cold concrete wall and tried to scan my history book. The words kept bouncing off my brain.

Finally, I turned to Ted or Thad, and said, "Like, if I couldn't go home tonight, do you know where I could spend the night?"

He gave me a go-away scowl.

"So it's all just for show, huh? That tough look?"

That needled him enough that he shrugged. "There's that place downtown. For homeless people. What's it called? Catholic Charities?"

I frowned. A shelter? That seemed kind of extreme, and, no offense, but it seemed kind of wrong to expect the Catholics to harbor a half vampire on the run from witches.

"Yeah, okay," I said, disappointed.

He looked at me, as though considering something. Then he said, "I know some guys, right. They squat in that big three-story house that's been for sale forever—you know the one, on the corner of Grotto?"

I did know the one. It was just up the street. I remembered it as a huge Federal-style house with columns and thick, granite bricks. I wasn't sure that was any safer than going to a shelter, but I was starting to feel like I had some options. "Thanks," I said gratefully.

"Don't mention it," he said, pulling his board up under his arm as the bus's brakes squealed to a stop in front of us. "But if you go, tell them Nate sent you."

"Nate." Okay, so not Ted. I thought I'd remember that if it became necessary. "Got it."

BEFORE THE FIRST BELL, TAYLOR was waiting at my locker. Ironically, someone had scrawled "Witch Bitch" in black Sharpie in large block letters on the red finish. "Wow," I said drily. "Look, apes know how to rhyme. We should call *Scientific American* or *National Geographic* or somebody."

In solidarity, Taylor smiled at my feeble joke. Today, her *hijab* was hot pink. She wore sparkly lipstick to match. Surprisingly, it looked awesome with her nut-brown skin. "With all the excitement about Nikolai, I kind of forgot about Thompson."

Hell, I'd forgotten about both.

"Did you bring Nik's CD?" Taylor asked hopefully. "I'd love to see it. Is it cool?"

"Yeah, it is," I said as I popped open the combination and started organizing my books for the day. Precalculus first period. What evil had I done to deserve math at nine o'clock in the morning? Math I could do, but first? Ugh.

"Sorry, things were kind of crazy this morning, and I left it at home," I told Taylor's anxious face. I left a ton of things I needed behind, like a toothbrush and a change of clothes. I couldn't seriously not go home tonight, could I?

"Yeah, say, how did your religious test go?"

"I flunked." Closing the locker, I stared at Thompson's poetry sullenly. It should really say "vamp tramp," since I wasn't a witch anymore. "Big-time."

"Oh. Well." She looked at her hands, which were twiddling. Then she brightened. "Hey, at least you got a boyfriend out of the deal."

Had I? "He hasn't called yet," I reminded her. "I'm not sure he will."

Taylor gave me a sidelong sly grin. "When he does—and he will—Bea is going to flip."

"Over what?" Bea stood beside Taylor and didn't even spare me a glance.

"Nikolai asked Ana out on a date," Taylor spilled excitedly.

I could have kicked her.

"Not yet. Not exactly," I mumbled. I expected Bea to turn on me in fury or horror, but she continued to talk only to Taylor. It was like I wasn't even there. What was this? Shunning?

"Nikolai Kirov?" Bea asked like we knew a ton of guys named Nikolai. "From my coven?"

Oh, it was *her* coven now, was it?

Taylor looked confused. She glanced at me for confirmation, but I was busy trying to force Bea to notice me by giving her the spooky eye. "Um, I guess," Taylor said. "I'm talking about the senior from last year who's in a metal band. That guy. The hottie."

Unbidden, the physical sensation of Nikolai's finger brushing the skin above my breast came back so strongly that I shivered. For the first time in my life, I had a sudden and deep desire to hurry to math class. "Yeah, well, you two talk among yourselves. I've got to go. The bell is going to ring any minute."

Bea looked at me then, and I thought she might say something. I wasn't sure I wanted to hear it, though. So I shouldered my bag and left the two of them standing by my vandalized locker gossiping about Nik or me or both. I actually couldn't wait for the mind-numbing experience that was precalc because I didn't want to think about any of this any more.

AFTER PRECALCULUS CAME GYM, a class I shared with Thompson. Did I mention the bad karma that was my schedule?

In the locker room, I changed into my shorts and T-shirt. Unfortunately, my fresh outfit was sitting on top of the laundry basket. In my hurry to flee from Mom, I completely forgot to grab it. All I had was the stinky crumple at the bottom of my backpack left over from last week. With a face, I got into it. At least everyone looked pretty miserable. We all marched into the gymnasium like prisoners heading into the yard for exercise.

Our gym teacher was Mr. Johnson. He was a thousand years old, perpetually grumpy, and the coach for football, naturally. He had us warm up for whatever hell he planned to put us through with a jog around the edge of the room, and a lot of drill-sergeant shouting about sissies. Thompson wasted no time coming up beside me and jabbing his elbow into my side.

Miraculously, I didn't stumble. It was kind of a weak effort on his part too, so I chided him sarcastically, "Is that the best you can do?"

To my surprise a couple of the other girls shouted, "Yeah!" and "Bully!" and "We saw what you did, jerk!"

I'd forgotten about the unpopularity spell. Thompson looked back at me with pure hatred burning in his eyes. I take it his day had sucked so far too. Alas, he probably planned to take it out on me. My day was going to suck even bigger.

As luck would have it, Thompson might have something else to expend his aggression on: floor hockey. I was actually kind of excited when I saw Mr. Johnson bring out the pucks and sticks; I wasn't half bad at floor hockey, myself.

Of course, first I had to endure the picking of sides, every unpopular kid's worst nightmare. One of Thompson's buddies got picked to captain team one. Some cheerleader got the other honor. I expected to be the last one standing, but as the names got called, I started to realize it was coming down to two: me and . . . Thompson.

And Thompson's buddy just called *my* name.

Holy shit.

Thompson looked ready to explode. He skulked over to the cheerleader's side, knuckles dragging.

Completely oblivious to Stassen High School history being made, Mr. Johnson called us to get started. We got our sticks, chose positions, and soon the puck went down. Despite the spell, Thompson took the part of goalie, a pretty good gig in my opinion.

At the whistle blow, furious scrabbling began. Since Thompson was stuck by the net, I kind of got into it. I let myself get lost in the game—the running, hooking, and passing the puck around the smooth polished floor.

I was almost having fun when Thompson's buddy slap-shot the puck high into the air. Like a true jock, Thompson stopped it from going into the net . . . with his face.

The flat plastic disk caught him hard on the scalp. Something crunched. Thompson swore up a blue streak. Blood splattered.

Action screeched to a halt. Everyone stared at the copious amount of blood coming from Thompson's head. It was clear the cut was superficial, but man, it was a gusher. I was close to the net, because I was expecting to help angle the puck into the goal. My nose twitched. I detected a strong odor of copper and salt.

And it smelled . . .

Tasty?

Thirteen

W hat happened next was one of the strangest moments in my life. I couldn't even tell you how I ended up holding Thompson's face in my hands with my palms gently cradling his cheeks. Or how my lips found their way to his bloody cheek . . .

The only thing I remember with any clarity was how hot his flesh felt beneath my own and the divine taste of his blood. The blood was exquisite, like the first time you experience chocolate— only better because it ignited all my senses. My nose was filled with its heady smell. My body trembled, flushing with excitement and desire. Time slowed and my vision seemed sharper, more focused. I felt incredibly alive.

And really, really hungry.

If Thompson hadn't pulled away in abject horror, I would have licked every drop from his face and then slurped the floorboards. . . .

Oh, my God.

I just, like, _tasted_ Thompson.

In front of everyone in gym.

Thompson stared at me. Mr. Johnson's mouth hung open in an ineffectual O. My arms were still open wide as if I wished to give Thompson a hug. Someone muttered about getting the janitor. The words broke the silence enough for people to begin to react. There were "ewww's" and "Gross!" and "Was she kissing him?" and "Look at all the blood."

I was looking all right. I was seriously considering licking my fingers, which had gotten smeared when I cradled Thompson's face.

So when the bell suddenly sounded, I fled.

Bolting into the locker room, I grabbed my bag and headed out the door. I didn't even bother to change. I was down the hall and out the door before the hall monitor could even shout a warning.

Outside, the cloud cover was heavy and dark. A mist had started falling, but still I ran. And running felt good. I mean, it wasn't just the pleasure of escape but the physical act that I enjoyed. My feet sped lightly over the uneven concrete of the sidewalk. It was as though my tennis shoes made the briefest contact before leaping skyward again. My heart pounded, but not uncomfortably. It was more like elation. I could have run like this forever.

I don't know how far my feet carried me, but I slowed when I saw a chain coffee shop. Its familiar logo shone like a beacon in the growing darkness. Thunder rolled. I ducked into the doorway just as the first large drops burst from the sky.

The comforting aroma of roasting coffee drew me farther inside. The place was relatively quiet, considering how many people sat at various tables sipping drinks and browsing on their laptops. Wi-Fi was free with a drink, or so the advertisement claimed. I made my way to the cashier.

"Name your poison," the barista said with a smile. She had an asymmetrical haircut and a ring through her nose like a bull. Tattoos snaked up both arms.

"Um, latte?"

I was still so out of it that she had to coach me through the whole Grande/Venti thing, but I eventually managed to place my order. As she handed me my change, she gave my outfit a once-over, but didn't comment, except to say, "The bathroom is straight back to the left."

As she started making my drink, I scurried to the restroom to change out of my bloody gym clothes. The bathroom lights buzzed and flickered for a second before snapping on to that harsh brightness of fluorescent. I had my shirt off when I caught my reflection in the mirror. The wind had blown my hair wild, and my eyes glittered like an animal's. In the strange light, my skin looked greenish; the smear of blood on my lips, black.

My tongue sought the errant blood, and I sucked it into my mouth greedily. For a second, the irises of my eyes refracted like a cat's.

I looked like a vampire—in gym shorts.

Hysterical laughter bubbled up, and I giggled until I realized exactly how crazy I looked. I wiped the remaining blood off my mouth with the back of my hand.

"What am I?" I asked the wild thing in the mirror. She just shook her head in mute confusion. I turned my back to my reflection and finished dressing. After stuffing my gym uniform into my backpack, I flicked off the light and shut the door without ever looking back.

Whoever that woman was in the mirror, I wasn't ready to deal with her. Not yet. I didn't even really know what it meant to be her. But my plan was simple. I was going to sit down, drink coffee, and try to put my head together. Then, I'd . . .

Okay, so I wasn't off to a very good start, because I didn't even know what I'd do after. Was I going to go home and risk Mom putting a spell on me to make me stay home? Or what? Be homeless?

My drink was ready, so I grabbed it and sat at a table where I could watch the rain. Drops had become sheets, and rivulets ran down the glass in squiggles. Watching their random patterns didn't offer any answers, but my breathing slowed and steadied.

I took a sip of coffee, expecting that sweet bitterness that I'd grown to love. It tasted like water. I almost spat it out. Even though I'd scrubbed them nearly raw, my fingers rose to my lips. The craving for blood lingered.

The door opened, bringing with it the scent of rain. My eyes flicked over the figure that came in, and then lingered on the smooth, graceful way he moved. Jeans clung wetly to long, slender legs. Thanks to the weather, the shirt he wore left little to the imagination, which was okay because I didn't think I could have come up with anything quite *that* good. When I looked up to see if he had a face to match, I was startled to see him looking at me.

"Elias!" I said, barely recognizing him with his clothes on. That thought brought a blush to my cheeks.

His smile was dazzling, and he did that odd little courtly nod with his hand briefly touching his heart. "May I join you, Your Highness?"

I nodded, but as he took the seat across from me, I regarded him with a bit of suspicion. After all, how likely was it that he was just passing by? On a day like this? Miles from where I'd seen him last? Twenty minutes after I'd, er, licked Thompson?

Also, according to the brightly colored clock on the wall, it was 11:36. Did that mean vampires could go out in daylight, or were the overcast clouds enough protection?

I'd ask him about the daylight thing later; first things first. "Are you stalking me?"

He laughed. On closer inspection, Elias was even hotter than I first thought. Apparently his eyes weren't permanently cat-slit, since today his pupils were round and the irises surrounding them were a pale, liquid green. He ran a hand through the short shock of hair on his head, giving it a sexy, tousled look. "Not exactly," he said with that high-wattage smile lingering on his face. "I was awakened by the blood."

My head hurt with the weird. I took a slow, thoughtful sip of coffee, trying to return to that steady place I'd been before. The bad-tasting coffee didn't help. "Are you saying you woke up out of your coffin when I—when that thing with Thompson happened?"

"Well, if you remove the coffin part, yes, basically."

Lightning made the overhead lights flicker slightly. A moment later thunder rattled the windows.

"You tasted blood for the first time. The entire clan felt it. Prince Ramses, your father, is very pleased, Your Highness," he continued. "His Highness regrets to inform you that he is unable to greet you on this auspicious moment personally. He sent me as his emissary. He's too old, you understand. The sun, it can reach him even through the rain. However, he would request your presence tonight for an official celebration."

"I'm kind of grounded. I'm supposed to go right home." I don't know why I blurted that out, since I hadn't been planning to go home anyway. But Elias's official speech sort of freaked me out. Even though I knew vampires were real, it just sounded so bizarre coming from this normal, good-looking guy sitting across from me at a Starbucks.

Elias's eyebrow shifted in an are-you-serious arch. "Grounded? No offense, Your Highness, but you're above all that now. More to the point, the invitation is tantamount to a royal summons. You really shouldn't blow that off. Besides, I believe it's meant to be your debut."

"My debut?"

"Your presentation to the clan, if you prefer. Your acceptance of your heritage. On the East Coast they call it a coming-out, but the connotation of that has changed over time, has it not?" He flashed a quirky smile.

Coming out as a vampire? Sort of like coming-out of the closet, only way, way weirder. "Yeah, it has." I smiled in return.

"So it is decided? You will come?" I shook my head. I mean, it all seemed so genteel, but, "I wouldn't know where to go or how to behave. I don't know anything about being a vampire."

His eyes flashed intensely as he spoke. "You know the most important thing. You know about the taste."

The taste . . . he didn't even have to explain of what. The second Elias mentioned it, I found myself craving blood like a drug. A shudder of a sigh escaped my lips.

He nodded approvingly at my reaction. I felt another blush growing, but he took my hand in his. He shifted to rest his elbows on the polished wood table. I was struck by how strong his body looked. In that way, it was easy to believe he was a knight.

He looked . . . dangerous. I could easily see him kicking Thompson's ass in a fight.

Or Nikolai's.

"About tonight . . . Your Highness, I would be at your side at every turn—if you so wished it. I could guide you, teach you our ways. You only need but ask."

The eyes that sought out mine held an intense fire. I felt strangely scrutinized, though it was far from unpleasant. My skin flushed and tingled. Trying to act cooler than I felt, I gave him a big teasing smile. "Are you asking me out?"

His smile faded suddenly, and his eyes dropped. He let go of my hand. "I would never presume."

What a cute reaction! It was totally seventeenth century.

"No, actually, it would be nice." I smiled.

He looked relieved. "Good. The festivities begin at sundown. Shall we arrange a place to meet?"

I raised my palms. "Hold on, Romeo. *If* I'm going to attend the debut, you can be my date. But I still haven't decided that I'm going. I mean, it's all kind of sudden, you know? I still can't believe I basically licked Thompson's face. What was I thinking?"

"You weren't. The blood is irresistible, especially blood of an enemy won in a fight."

That sounded far too noble to describe what had happened, so I reminded him: "It was floor hockey."

"He was your opponent at least?"

One of the machines behind the coffee bar made a whooshing noise, loud enough to preclude conversation momentarily. "Yeah, I guess so. We were on opposite sides, but . . . it was just gym class." Elias looked at me like he sensed there was more to it, so I admitted, "Okay, Thompson and I have been going back and forth, you know, since the whole stupid scene in the lunch-room when I gave him the spooky eye, but enemies? I don't know. I guess. But that seems harsh."

"Whatever happened, the circumstances satisfied the ritual of the hunt. Nothing less than first blood would have awoken us."

I didn't know what to say to that, so I played with the plastic top of my drink. "First blood? Does that mean I'm a vampire now?"

He looked vaguely offended momentarily, but then quickly recovered his expression. "You have always been what you are, my lady," he said curtly. Then he stood up. "I'm going to get something to drink. You want anything?"

I shook my head. Well, that answered another question I had: at least as a vamp I didn't have to give up my coffee. Apparently vampires could drink something other than blood. Not that anything else would ever taste as good.

Crap, listen to me. I sounded like a bloodsucker. I wondered what Nikolai would think of me now. Had I crossed some line with this whole first-blood thing? Would the Elder Witches open hunting season on me?

I guess I could kiss a bowling date good-bye if that happened, huh?

With a steaming mug of what looked like plain, black coffee, Elias resumed his seat across from me. Other than his on-the-pale-side skin, there wasn't much about him that screamed vampire. His hair was cut short and stylishly—very "now." The shirt he wore could have been picked up at any department store yesterday, and a funky gold cross gleamed at the hollow of his throat.

A cross?

Okay, it didn't look like the standard Christian cross that a lot of kids at school wore. It had a few extra bits, and I thought it might be Greek or Russian Orthodox, but I couldn't be sure.

I pointed to it. "So crosses don't burn your skin."

"Not here," he said casually, like that explained everything.

As I watched him take a sip from his cup, all sorts of questions bubbled through my head. "So before . . . you said my dad couldn't come himself because he's too old? Are you saying that it gets harder for vampires to go out in the daylight as they age?"

"Light has always been the enemy of the dark realm. Sensitivity to it grows with time."

"Huh. So . . . how old are you?"

"Older than you. Significantly."

I probably shouldn't have, but I had to laugh. "Well, you don't look it."

He tipped his head in acknowledgment. "Thanks."

"You say that I am what I've always been, but what the hell is that?"

A strangely devilish smile turned up his lip slightly. "Funny you should mention hell."

Fourteen

There was something about the look in his eye that drew a chill up my spine. I swallowed, but my throat was dry as I repeated, "Hell?"

"It's a misconception, of course. Most of us are far older than the concepts of heaven and hell. But even we have forgotten much about the place we were stolen from. All that remains has become so entangled with your images and associations with Hades as to be indistinguishable."

I tried to remember to breathe as Elias spoke. What had my mother called my dad? "Demon." Did she mean that literally? Was I half . . . devil?

And what was I supposed to make of that? I didn't even believe in demons and hell. Of course, yesterday I didn't believe in vampires either.

Elias watched my eyes for a second before continuing. "The history of our exile is murky, but the old ones tell us that the First Witch broke through the barrier between our worlds. In order to practice real magic, she drew her power from the other side, our home."

I couldn't take it. I had to interrupt. "Wait a minute—are you saying magic actually comes from Satan?"

"No, as I said, this happened in a time long before Christianity. Before Yahweh. Before writing. But magic, the magic your people practice, draws on the energy of that place beyond the veil, my homeland, your hell."

"I can't believe it," I said. "You realize what you're saying is every Wiccan's nightmare, right?"

"I know." He looked away, watching the storm shake the leaves from the trees. The muscle of his jaw worked furiously as he tried to find the words. "But try to rise above the human tendency to paint everything with simple, broad strokes, my lady. Your father passed through the veil long before Christ walked the earth. People have always been afraid of what lies beyond. When the First Witch stole the first prince from our homeland, there was no word for what we were. Almost every culture has one now: djinn, devil, demon, *oni*, *nephilim*, *grigori*, *púca*, *wyrm*. . . . Whatever evil has tormented mankind from the moment Pandora's box was opened . . . has been attributed to our race."

"Evil?" I breathed, remembering the glint in my own eye that I'd seen in the bathroom.

He shook his head. "Evil is, even for us, a choice. That is, unless we are being compelled by magic."

"Compelled? I don't get it. The First Witch brought vampires . . . or whatever, through from the other side, okay, sure. But I don't understand—why?"

"To be her slaves."

Slaves? He made it sound so matter-of-fact, like I might have learned of it in grade school along with the "golden triangle." But he was suggesting that those revered ancestors of mine in the great Book of Shadows had kept vampire-demons as slaves.

I felt blindsided by this knowledge on so many levels. I'd always scoffed at the account of the confessions by witches under torture in *Malleus Maleficarum*. But countless victims of the Inquisition had told of demon slaves, minions from hell. Had those stories been true?

And Nikolai had mentioned something about a residual binding spell used to capture and kill vampires. Was this what he referred to?

I didn't know, but at the very least, this history might explain why vampires and witches didn't get along. "But you're not slaves anymore . . . uh, or are you?"

"We have not been compelled to do witch bidding since the Burning Times, when, during the great cull, the talisman the First Witch created to bind us was stolen and hidden, to be lost forever." And then he added something in a language I didn't understand and rapped his knuckles on the table, like some kind of superstitious ritual.

I considered everything as I took another sip of the dreadful coffee. Elias had also said that real magic drew on the essence of the other side, the dark realm, the place he and his people had come from. "If real magic is made from the stuff of your homeland, why can't you use it?"

"It is our life force, much like your blood. We can no more make magic from our essence than you can with yours."

Now my head was really spinning with the realization: "Witches feed on your 'blood,' and you drink ours. Holy shit."

He chuckled a bit. " 'Holy'? Perhaps 'infernal.' "

"No," I said. " 'Infernal shit' just doesn't have the right sound, trust me."

We shared a smile and it might have been some kind of moment between us, except the door opened, letting in a gust of moist air and a gaggle of giggling girls. I sort of recognized one of them as being from Stassen; she was part of what Bea and I dubbed the stoner clique. You know the sort, always skipping school and getting caught smoking on school grounds? Our eyes met, and she gave me a brief glare.

I turned back to Elias, who was sipping his coffee and noticing how I reacted as the girls noisily made their way up to the counter. He seemed more on alert, as though he might leap up to defend my honor at any moment.

"It's okay, sir knight, you can sheath your sword," I teased him. "They're just some kids from school."

He gave me an acknowledging, militarist lift of the chin, as though I'd given him an order to obey.

"What *is* the deal with all the court stuff? I mean, how is it that my dad is a prince when you guys were slaves?"

"Ah," he said, taking a moment to study his hands encircling the coffee mug before he answered. "What do you know of medieval Christian demonology?"

"Zero?"

"Well, it's based largely on what we remember of our stations in the dark realm. We've always strictly adhered to it. It's what remains of our culture."

The girls from school noisily descended on a table near us. Book bags banged and they harassed one another jokingly at a high decibel. It distracted me from the conversation with Elias.

One of the girls—I thought her name might be Violet or Ruby—noticed me. "What are you looking at, witch?"

I shrugged and looked away guiltily.

Elias, however, had turned to stare steadily at the speaker until she was forced to drop her hostile gaze in return.

"Don't engage them," I whispered to Elias, but it was too late. I could feel my anger building, almost like magic, bubbling just under the surface ready to explode. I don't know why they bothered me so much; maybe I was looking for an excuse to vent some of the frustration I felt about all this crazy vampire stuff.

The girls were whispering among themselves and pointing at me. They were snickering in a way that was clearly unkind and cruel. One of them piped up with, "Aren't you that girl that kissed that jock during gym? He says you licked the blood off his nose. Are you some kind of fetishist or something?"

I opened my mouth to tell them to shut up and mind their own business, but all that came out was a catlike hiss. My mouth felt strange too, like it had gotten too small for all my teeth.

The stoner-clique girls' eyes went wide. Their expressions were a study in stunned horror. Then, as if someone had pulled the fire alarm, they scattered, barely taking the time to grab all their drinks and go.

When I tried to ask Elias what had just happened, I nicked my tongue on sharp points of my teeth.

Fangs?

Where had they come from?

Fifteen

y jaw clicked and shifted. As unexpectedly as they had appeared, my fangs retracted and were gone. I cautiously ran my tongue around my mouth, but there was no trace of sharpness. The copper taste of my own blood filled my mouth, but it wasn't anything like the addictive deliciousness I'd begun to associate with bleeding.

Elias watched me curiously. "I see my lady can protect herself quite admirably," he said drily, but a smile played on his face. "However, perhaps in the future, Her Highness might consider diplomacy first?"

I was too upset to be amused by his teasing response. I mean, I'd just hissed at my classmates like a feral cat. How was that even remotely normal?

I stood up on shaky feet. "Yeah, uh, you know what? I want to go home."

And I suddenly did, very much. Hiding under the covers sounded like a pleasant solution to all of this crazy.

Elias rose the second I did. "As you wish." He tipped his head slightly. "Allow me to accompany you." When I hesitated, he added, "I have a car. It'll save you a long, wet walk in the rain."

"You have a car?" I don't know why, but it struck me as very odd that this guy whom I'd seen leaping around in the trees naked owned something as everyday as a car.

"Public transportation in this city leaves a lot to be desired."

In other words, it sucked. "Yeah, true enough," I agreed. "Okay, why not?"

LIKE A TRUE GENTLEMAN, ELIAS offered to bring the car around to the front entrance of the coffee shop so I'd only have to make a quick dash out into the rain. I stood outside under the awning, straining to see his headlights. As I waited, a woman with an umbrella headed toward the door. I stepped out of her way with a mumbled apology.

Instead of reaching for the handle, she grabbed my wrist.

"Hey!" I shouted.

In the murky light, I saw her cat-slit eyes glinting. A vampire! With a quick flick of her arm, the umbrella collapsed closed. She raised it as though she meant to skewer me with the pointy tip of the shaft.

I screamed in anticipation of the blow, twisting awkwardly out of the way when she brought the umbrella down. The sharp tip skimmed past my waist.

Instinctively, my fangs dropped, but they didn't do much for me other than make my mouth feel too full. So I kicked her knee.

To my great surprise, my foot connected and she stumbled backward.

A car pulled up to the curb. I lunged for it. My sneakers slapped on the wet pavement. I ran without looking to see if my attacker was in pursuit.

The instant the door opened, I scooted in. Elias peeled out into traffic before I had my safety belt strapped. In the side mirror, I saw the umbrella-wielding woman pulling herself to her feet with a creepy deliberation; her eyes seemed to find mine despite the distance rapidly increasing between us.

"She attacked me!" I said, even though it was patently obvious. "Who was that?"

"One of the loyal opposition," Elias said. His vehicle appeared to be some kind of luxury car. It had all the latest features and silver, new-smelling upholstery. I resisted the urge to pull my dripping wet sneakers up off the rug.

"There's a civil war brewing," Elias continued. "Some of the exiles from the dark realm still prefer the simplicity of slavery to the complexities of freedom. They prefer to follow old masters, even if not compelled to do so."

The disdain in his voice made it easy for me to figure out which side he was on.

"You've been free for centuries," I said. "Shouldn't everyone, you know, have adjusted by now?"

"We were slaves for millennia."

Some kind of belly-dancing music played softly on the MP3 player, which was the only part of this scene that felt right to me. Elias was a relaxed and comfortable driver, but he looked alien amid all this gleaming technology. He'd look better, I thought, deep in the branches of some ancient oak and, ahem, naked.

"Are you all right?" he asked once we'd put several blocks behind us. And for a second, I thought he might have sensed my elevated heart rate at the thought of him without his clothes on, but he added, "She didn't injure you, did she?"

I didn't think so. I checked my shirt. There was a small tear in the side, but nothing more serious.

"You and your father are at the heart of this conflict, you know," Elias said, giving me a quick glance before returning his attention to the rain-slicked streets. "Not long ago, Prince Ramses led the Concessionists. He negotiated a peace treaty between the exiles and the oppressors." He coughed, and then clarified, "I mean, the witches."

"So there's peace?"

"No. The treaty was a sham. We were betrayed." His eyes narrowed darkly as he glared angrily at the road. My mouth opened to ask more, but he pulled the car in front of my house.

I blinked. He'd had no trouble at all finding my place. Even Nikolai and I had driven past it twice. "But the wards . . . ?"

Elias understood my question instantly. "My prince's blood stains your threshold, my lady. More than that, you are his blood. The befuddlement spell is no match for such a marker."

"Oh," was all I could think to say. I had my hand on the door latch. I glanced between my house and Elias. "So, uh, do you want to come in? I just want to grab a few things. Then maybe we could, like, go out to lunch or something."

"The invitation is generous, but I can't count on this rain to last," he said, peering at the dark wall of clouds. "I'll need to return underground soon."

"Seriously?"

"Quite."

*   *   *

So I left Elias waiting in the car, especially after he explained that my mom would likely sense another trespasser of his "caliber," whatever that meant exactly, on her doorstep. It was enough for me to know that Mom's Spidey-sense would tingle if Elias came in.

I did *not* want to alert Mom. Especially since on top of everything else, I was now officially truant from school.

Pulling my schoolbooks out of my backpack, I dumped them on the parson's bench. With the whole Thompson licking incident, I knew I wasn't going back to school today. I just couldn't face it. My cell tumbled out and bounced on the floor. Picking it up, I thumbed it on.

The screen danced with missed calls, voice mail, and text messages. I must have had three dozen! Just scanning the titles of the texts, however, I knew most of them could wait. Everyone wanted details about gym class. Taylor was the only one to ask if I was okay. There was nothing, not even a gossipy taunt, from Bea.

I quickly wrote Taylor back just to reassure her I was . . . mostly. I told her I'd call after school, if I got a chance.

To Bea, I couldn't resist a sarcastic, "Glad you care so much."

My finger hesitated over the send button. Should I let her know how much she hurt me? She seemed to be just fine with acting like I didn't exist. Maybe I should pretend I didn't care either.

I still wore the necklace she'd given me yesterday. I could feel all the care she'd put into it resonating from the stones. If she wanted to pretend our friendship didn't matter to her, fine. But that's all it was: pretend.

I hit SEND.

And I took the necklace off. I thought about tossing it on the floor, but I just couldn't. So I stuffed it into the outer pocket of my backpack.

Quickly, I dashed upstairs to gather a few things. I had no idea what a person was supposed to wear to her debut as a vampire princess, so along with some utilitarian stuff like socks and underwear, I pulled out my nicest sundress, nylons, and matching heels. From the bathroom I gathered my toiletries, some makeup, bits of my favorite jewelry, and Mom's sandalwood perfume. I paused before tossing it into my bag, but it wasn't as if I was stealing it. I'd be back . . . eventually.

What else?

Money.

Back in my room, I frantically dug through my dresser drawer until I found my collection of gift cards. Many of my extended relatives, especially those who weren't witches, didn't know what to give me for birthdays or holidays, so I'd amassed a fat wad of no-expiration-date gift cards for everything from Barnes & Noble to Home Depot.

Alas, the only other cash I had was my penny jar, which was really an old pot I'd picked up at an antiques store that I tossed my change into. Even though it probably had twenty or thirty bucks in it, it was far too heavy to bring along.

I had no idea what else might be important, so I whispered a quiet, heartfelt "Good-bye" and bounded down the stairs with my overflowing backpack. Somewhere deep inside the jumble of jammed clothing and such, my cell rang.

Ignoring it for now, I rifled through the hall closet until I found a waterproof jacket. I lifted the lace curtain by the parson's bench to check to see if Elias was still there. I could see the silver drops of rain reflected in his headlights beyond the shrubbery and fence. Shrugging into the jacket, I clutched my backpack. As the call rang into voice mail, I remembered to lock the door and ran out to the warmth of the waiting car.

"Where shall we go, my lady?"

Even though it was horribly old-fashioned, my heart still skipped a beat when Elias called me his lady. I watched the raindrops spatter the window. Were they slower now? Would the sun be out soon? I didn't want Elias to be hurt, so I said:

"Underground?"

Sixteen

was glad I hadn't changed into my sundress when Elias showed me the sewer manhole.

The rain had slowed considerably by the time we parked in the Swede Hollow neighborhood. The cloud cover was breaking up. Rain had changed from sheets to a miserable light drizzle that ran down the collar of my coat and plastered my hair flat against my face.

"You're kidding, right?"

The residential block was deserted; apparently most people in the area worked nine to five. Elias squatted in the middle of the empty street, prying the manhole cover off with a crowbar he'd retrieved from his trunk. I leaned against the door of the car with my arms crossed in front of my chest. My head shook in dismay and disbelief.

Okay, I didn't know what to expect when I suggested we go underground, but I'd gotten it into my head that vampires were natural creatures. The last place I expected Elias to take me was to a sewer drain.

"You aren't seriously expecting me to go down into *there*."

Elias had the cover off and pushed to one side. For a moment, he regarded me with a hint of wounded pride. "There's more underground than rat tunnels, my lady. If you would but follow me, you shall see."

I could smell the distinctive smell of treated waste even from a distance. "No way."

With a quick look up at the lightening sky, he deftly lowered himself in. "The time has come for me to return. You must do as you wish, of course, Your Highness. But whatever you choose, pray do so quickly."

It would be a long, wet walk home. Besides, I couldn't really go home . . . not tonight, anyway. I was still worried that Mom might decide to magically ground me, as it were. That scared me, especially now that I knew that vampires were easily enslaved by witches. Would I even know if she put me under?

I shuddered at the thought of the gross damp tunnels, but I said, "Fine, I'm coming."

With a nod, Elias began his descent.

Just below the mouth of the slender hole, a ladder disappeared into the darkness. In less than a foot or so, it was so pitch-black that I couldn't see any sign of Elias. I knelt by the opening and peered down. "Uh, hello?"

I nearly jumped when Elias's face materialized out of the blackness. "Please, my lady. Let us make haste." Then he was gone again.

"But I can't see."

His disembodied voice echoed in the musty, dank air wafting from the hole. "I will guide you. Hurry, we can't be seen coming this way."

Did I need to shut the door, as it were, behind us? I looked at the heavy manhole cover. I tried to move it, but no matter how hard my muscles strained to lift the cover, it didn't budge. "I can't get it."

"I will send the Cerberus to hide our tracks." Soft clanging footfalls retreated deeper.

I didn't want to be left too far behind, so I finally made my move. Tentatively, I put a foot on the first rung. It felt far too slender and slippery, and the hole seemed way too deep and dark. I held my breath and grabbed the top with my hand.

As I started down, I looked up. The sky was a gray circle surrounded by black. My knees trembled. "I don't like this." My voice sounded even shakier and weak.

"Just keep climbing. It's not far."

Despite his assurances, it became hard for me to release each foot to the surrender of that horrible moment of nothingness between steps—especially now that the shadows had completely surrounded me and I could see nothing. It was like dropping down a ladder with your eyes closed. Only worse, because no matter what I did, I still couldn't see where I was going.

"I don't know if I can do this," I said. When I looked up, the fading gray sky of the exit was no larger than a doughnut. My stomach twisted and turned into shivering knots. My knees locked. I couldn't go farther down and, instead, had to fight the urge to scramble back up the way I'd come.

Light flared below me. Suddenly, I could see that I stood on the final rung, which was situated about a foot above the floor. I hopped down quickly, thankful for solid ground. The tunnel had opened up to a large, hand-hewn sandstone passage. A set of railroad tracks ran down the center.

Elias held a flashlight with a wide beam. Swinging it around to illuminate the wall I'd just climbed down, he indicated a shelf that had been placed near the ladder and that was filled with various sizes and shapes of flashlights. I gasped when I noticed the young, pale-faced, dark-eyed boy sitting silently in the ratty wicker chair beside it. His dark hair fell in lanky strands. The dark pits of his eyes watched me, unblinking.

"Your Highness, this is a Cerberus. He guards the gate," Elias said as the young man stood and bowed in my direction.

"Um, hi," I said.

The boy nodded again. Taking a flashlight from the pile, he handed it to me. I took it. With another bob of his head, the boy scrambled up the ladder.

"Won't the sunlight bother him?" I asked.

"He's human," Elias said simply. Perhaps in the dark Elias could see my stricken expression, because he added, "He's well looked after. Better here than above, at any rate. From time to time, we take in strays—people that otherwise have no place—and in exchange, they guard us while we're vulnerable and asleep." Elias pointed his flashlight down the tracks. "Now, if you'll follow me?"

Well, I'd come this far, hadn't I?

Switching on the flashlight the strange boy had offered, I followed as Elias walked along the tracks. I flashed the light around the chamber, surprised how high the ceiling was. At intervals, thick beams of dark wood reinforced the tunnel.

I was glad I had my coat. The underground air was chilly and damp. The smell I'd associated with the sewer was fainter here, though water glistened on the tan sandstone, making the walls appear dusted with a fine spray of glitter.

We moved along the passage without speaking. Something about the space brought on a reverent silence. Sounds of scrabbling on stone echoed and rebounded in the cavernous dark. I swung my flashlight around trying to see what it was. When a bat flitted past my head, I squeaked in fright, nearly tripping in the gravel-strewn areas between the ties.

Elias laughed kindly, and his hand lightly grasped my elbow to steady me. "We have long shared our daylight living spaces with bats," he said. "Hence the association."

I smiled like I appreciated the information, but all I could think was *Ewww!*

Bats flashed in and out of the beams of our lights, and I did my best not to flinch. Ahead, I heard a gentle gurgling sound. With a brief touch on my shoulder, Elias directed me toward a more natural opening in the wall. We stepped off the tracks and ducked through the entrance. The inside revealed an odd scene. A creek flowed between sandy banks. Frogs peeped on the shoreline. They plopped into the water with a splash as we walked along the edge of the water.

"This is cool," I breathed. The air smelled fresher. Only a hint of the moldy darkness marred the air.

The walls of this new cave were a combination of river-cut sandstone and industrial debris. The ceiling would have felt more like a cavern's except for the rebar, steel beams, and broken concrete that formed an artificial roof. Occasionally the walls rumbled and shook with the sound of traffic passing overhead.

Elias continued to lead me along the banks of the underground river. Once again I was startled by the appearance of a sentry who stepped out of the shadows and blocked our path. Her long stringy hair appeared almost white and her eyes bulged slightly, reminiscent of those blind albino cave fish. She wore khaki hiking shorts, combat boots, and a tank top underneath an army surplus jacket. When she saw Elias, she snapped a smart salute and all but clicked her heels.

"Sir!"

"At ease," Elias said after returning her salute. "I present Her Highness Anastasija Ramses Parker. We request entrance to the city."

"Granted," the guard said. "Welcome back, Captain."

She smiled and then the two of them clasped hands. To me, Elias said, "I'm afraid there won't be much to see. The court sleeps."

THE PASSAGE WIDENED. STALACTITES DRIPPED from above, creating graceful, latticelike patterns. In these various nooks and crannies people slept.

I'll be honest—they didn't look entirely human. There was something animalistic in the way they huddled together. Men and women slept partly on top of one another, and most were quite naked. Their pale bodies gleamed like deposits of alabaster.

"The exile court of the dark realm," Elias said formally, gesturing in the direction of a platform formation I had not initially noticed. A waterfall split around a tall outcropping. In the center, between the twin sprays, a man sat on an indentation as though it were a throne.

"Dad?" I asked, recognizing the figure. I took a step closer and shone my light directly at his face. It was him all right. He wore fancy clothes and was wrapped in a purple cloak. His eyes stared forward, and I thought he must see me, so I waved. Elias shook his head. "His Highness is indisposed. The sleep has reclaimed him."

"Oh." My voice was small. I shone my light around at all the sprawling, naked bodies. Everyone seemed to have fallen into heaps, like victims of some horrible plague or nuclear disaster. "Aren't they cold?"

"No, we're impervious to temperatures of all kinds."

"Oh." I toed the soft sand ground. "So this is where you live?"

He glanced around as if trying to see how the place must look to me. "Yes," he said finally. "I know it's difficult to imagine, but it has its beauty. Tonight you shall see this transformed into a glittering palace, alive with laughter and delight."

He was right about one thing: I couldn't picture it. What he described sounded lovely, but what I saw now was kind of disturbing.

"The sleep calls to me as well, my lady," he said. "Soon I'll be of little use to you."

"You're taking a nap? Now?" I was horrified at the thought of being abandoned among all these lifeless vampires.

He looked stricken. "I must."

"Please stay awake with me, Elias."

"I'll do what I can," he said. Taking my hand, he brought me to a spot near where we'd first entered. He sat down on the ground, with his back against the cave wall. After a brief hesitation, I took off my backpack and set it on the sandy floor. I perched uncomfortably on top of it. The spot he'd chosen hid the view of most of the cadaverous court.

Elias's eyelids drooped, but he fought to keep them open. I snuggled next to him, sensing the heat of his body.

Was this the life I had to look forward to as a vampire? Sleeping naked in a cave during the day?

"Do you like being . . . what you are?"

"Hmmm?" Elias asked sleepily.

I lifted my hands to indicate the cave and its inert inhabitants. "Do you like your life?"

But he didn't answer. He'd fallen fast asleep.

I SAT FOR A WHILE with my butt getting colder, feeling kind of stupid and bored. What time was it? I wondered. Out of my bag, I retrieved my cell phone. It was nearly three. The final bell would be ringing soon. There were no signal bars—no surprise, I supposed, given how far we had to be underground. I scrolled through my messages anyway. Most of them were from people I knew only tangentially.

There was a text I hadn't noticed. It was from Nikolai. He wanted to go out tonight. Talk about a dilemma! Stay here with the unconscious vamps and have my debut at the exile court, or go bowling with a hottie rocker witch whose family hunted people like this?

Elias huffed quietly in his sleep. Water dripped from the dank-smelling walls.

Sitting here pretty much sucked.

But could I find my way back?

First, I dug out a notepad and a pen from the front pocket of my backpack. My pen hovered over the half-sized page I tore out. What to write? "Sorry. Had to go, got better offer" might be accurate, but it was hardly kind. "Dead naked people not my scene. Went bowling" sounded too flippant. I mean, I was giving up my supposed "debut" to go off on a date with Nikolai, and it wasn't Elias's fault I found this cave-sleeping part of vampirism unsettling.

In the end I settled on not giving any kind of explanation. I wrote simply, "Sorry," and left my phone number and my name. "Will see you tonight as promised."

I had no idea if Elias even owned a cell, but he'd surprised me with the car. I felt a small pang as I tucked the note between his fingers, which were laced on his chest. Elias deserved more, but I couldn't condense my feelings in a short note. Everything had happened so quickly. Only yesterday I found Thompson annoyingly cute. Today, I tried to eat him. And grew fangs. Sitting in a cave under St. Paul surrounded by dead-looking people was *not* what I needed.

I probably should have gone back to school when Elias asked where I wanted to go. I could have used the steadiness of my normal routine. Unfortunately, it was too late for that now.

I ducked through the narrow passage to where the sentry waited. She frowned at my approach. "Who goes there?" she actually asked.

"Anastasija Ramses Parker," I said, trying to sound authoritative as I added, "Vampire princess."

We stared at each other. I waited for her to step out of my way so I could slip past, but she didn't. Was I supposed to ask for permission to leave? I wondered if she was human, like the boy, and if I could push her out of the way if need be. "Uh, I need to go," I said.

She frowned. I'd obviously muffed protocol, but she nodded and stepped aside. "As you wish, Your Highness."

I slid past her, with a nod of acknowledgment.

She stuck her head into the passageway as though looking for something else. "No escort?"

"He's asleep," I explained. To her skeptical look, I added, "I'll be okay. Anyway, I'll be back."

She seemed on the verge of protesting, but I could see from her expression she was torn. Clearly, she had to guard the cave, but she didn't like me leaving, particularly on my own. Eventually, she shrugged. "Godspeed, Your Highness."

"Uh, thanks," I murmured as I began retracing our steps.

Luckily, our feet had made tracks in the sandy riverbank. I shone my beam on them. Once again, I was struck by how much like a natural river the underground stream looked. Its edges snaked to and fro, and the walls of the surrounding cave were more like cliffs, rising straight upward. In places, the wall jutted outward and I had to hang on to the stone to avoid stepping in the water.

I came to the turnoff. Crawling through that hole brought me back to the railroad tracks. I'd been hoping to follow our footprints, but to my dismay, I discovered trails leading both ways. Had we come from the right or left? My sense of direction was pretty good as long as I had the sun to steer by. In the dark, I was completely disoriented.

I'd just have to guess. At least I remembered we hadn't come far. If I didn't come across creepy boy with the flashlights soon, I'd turn around and backtrack.

I tried not to remember the stories of the kids who died after being lost in the Wabasha caves. Seemed like every year the

Pioneer Press reported about some idiots who'd gone in urban spelunking never to return. Of course, now I wondered, had they come across a vampire lair and been dispatched by a sentry? After all, some of the bodies were never found.

As I walked, the quality of light seemed to change. It appeared grayer, more infused with sun. Conversely, the air had grown heavy with a foul, sour scent, like human urine. Shining my light on the walls revealed gang-style graffiti. The ground was littered with abandoned beer bottles, cigarette stubs, aluminum cans, and other more disgusting, less identifiable garbage. I knew I'd taken a wrong turn, and was about to head back when I heard a loud rattle and whine of a diesel engine. Other traffic noises followed, along with a fresh burst of city-scented breeze.

I must be coming to an alternate exit. I decided to press on, at least as far as the turn up ahead. If I could see a way out from there, I'd take it. The turn revealed a split in the tracks. One tunnel disappeared back under the city; the other led to sunlight. The only problem? The exit was blocked by an iron fence, with bars shaped like a grid.

Undeterred, I inspected the fence. After all, it was obvious by the graffiti and other trash that people had come this way before. Sure enough, someone had loosened the bottom corner. I was able to tug the rusty section aside. I wouldn't fit with my backpack, but with some clever maneuvering I was able to pull it through after me. Of course, where I'd had to shimmy on my belly, my clothes now stank of . . . something I tried really hard not to think about.

Gross!

I shook myself out as best as possible and scrammed out into fresh air, such as it was. I'd come out somewhere near Lowertown, near the rail yards. It still drizzled slightly, and the sky remained a disheartening gray. The traffic sounds were coming from the Mound's View Bridge far overhead as tires hissed on the rain-drenched asphalt. The railroad stretched along the banks of a valley nestled among sandstone cliffs. Empty train cars sat on the tracks, their sides festooned with crass urban art. Sandpipers skipped along the tracks, and pigeons burst into flight in excited, chaotic circles at every noise. A barge horn sounded from the Mississippi, which was visible between the cars.

I headed in the direction of the river. I knew Shepard Road or one of those other streets dipped down into this strange no-person's land between downtown and the East Side. Mom had accidentally taken us here once when we were trying to get to the science museum's entrance.

It was going to be a long hike. Though I could see the road, it was a ways up into downtown. At least I could catch a city bus there. When I'd decided not to go for my driver's license, I made sure to get a monthly bus pass. As I walked, I flipped open my phone. Finally, bars!

The first person I replied to was Nikolai. I said yes and asked for details. Oh, and could he pick me up somewhere that wasn't home? I explained I was fighting with Mom.

Then, I asked Taylor how the rest of the day was going at school. Was I a total outcast now? Did she think I could ever show my face?

To the rest of the curious nonclose friends, I tried to decide how to "spin" the Thompson incident. I mean, maybe there was a way to explain it that wouldn't involve the word "vampire" or a plea of temporary insanity.

Maybe I should cop to my crush on him? Would people believe I kissed him out of kindness and then got so embarrassed I ran away? I nodded to myself as I dashed across the street to the steep sidewalk. My legs strained at the steep incline as I replied to everyone with the same lie.

Sure, I felt dishonest, but, look, no one would believe me if I told them the truth: I licked Thompson's tasty blood because I found out last night that I'm half vampire, and a princess no less! No way. Would you believe that?

Anyway, I could suffer the ribbing I'd get for being the dorky geek-freak who swooned over a dumb jock. It was the sort of thing that was expected in high school. Being a vampire? Not so much.

Especially when part of being a vampire involved naked cave sleeping. It seemed kind of creepy and alien. Maybe as a half vamp I could be excused from the nudist spelunking? I glanced up at the sky. Afternoon had always been my low point, biorhythmically speaking, but I didn't feel compelled to sleep the day away.

At least I never had in the past.

Of course, before today, I'd never sprouted fangs either.

Finally, I reached the top of the steep hill, which brought me to the lowest part of downtown St. Paul. Hotels and office buildings stretched skyward. White-collar workers huddled near back doors on smoke breaks. I walked up toward the main post office, passing under a covered bridge made of stone. I never knew what it was for or if it was still in use, but it looked like an early attempt at a skyway, though I thought maybe it was left over from the days when this part of the city was a more bustling port, perhaps to transfer cargo or goods to rail or shipping lines.

Rain misted my face. I shrugged deeper into my jacket. I checked my phone for the time. School was just about out. I wondered what Bea was doing, and if Mr. Martinez had noticed my absence. Would Taylor and Bea still meet at her locker? What would they talk about?

Just then, a text appeared from Bea. The sound of it ringing through nearly made me drop the phone. Talk about spooky timing. I was just thinking about her. Of course, it could be more than a coincidence. It could be magic. She was a full True Witch now. Maybe she'd sensed my thoughts?

I stared at the phone. Should I open it? How mad was she? Although at least she wasn't completely shunning me—that was good, right?

The light changed, so I dashed across the wide, four-lane street. I wasn't sure I was up to Bea drama right now, so I shoved the phone into my pocket.

Dark skies reflected off gray buildings. I stuffed my hands into the pockets of my raincoat trying to warm them.

I thought about Nikolai. I knew he was a freshman at the university studying, what? Was it music? Or something like business? I couldn't remember now, but I knew he had an apartment with some other college students. Had he gotten my message? Did he really want to go out with me tonight?

My mom was probably coming home for a late lunch before heading off for her St. Thomas class. Had she noticed the missing stuff? Had school called to report me truant?

As if in answer to my question, the phone rang. It was Nik. More magic summoning?

"Hey," I said, trying to sound cool and not out of breath when I answered.

"Hey, yourself." His voice sounded warm and familiar. I found myself smiling at the sound of it. "I got your text. I can pick you up anywhere. What's going on with your mom?"

The nice thing about Nikolai was that I didn't have to lie to him about anything. "This whole half-vampire thing has her freaked-out. I sensed her trying to put a compulsion spell on me this morning to try to keep me under house arrest until next full moon. She wants me to try the Initiation again."

"That's crazy," he agreed. "So what are you going to do?"

"I don't know. But I'm glad you want to do something to-night. I, uh, could really use someone to talk to."

"Where are you? Do you want to come over now and hang out?"

Did I ever! "That would be great."

NIKOLAI PULLED UP NEXT TO the bus stop. With a self-conscious look at the other people waiting, I scooted into his car. He had the heat on to defog the windshield, but it felt divine compared with the wet chill outside. I buckled in and he took off with a rat-tling roar.

"Thanks for picking me up," I said, wedging my backpack between my knees.

He gave me a stern look, like he was trying to be professorial or parental—which so did not work with those dark lashes and liquid gold eyes. "Should I ask why you're not at school?"

Did I explain to the vampire hunter about Thompson? "No?"

That surprised him, and his teasing smile disappeared. "Oh. Okay."

Now I felt bad. I chewed my fingernail. "It's a vampire thing," I said cautiously.

"And you don't want to tell me because I'm a hunter, right?" I nodded.

The car moved in stops and starts through downtown. There weren't a lot of cars on the street, but the lights were badly timed. We'd get started just in time to slow for the next intersection. He didn't say anything for a long time. The windshield wipers beat out a slow tempo.

"Ever since the Initiation, my dad has been pushing me to ramp up my training," he said. "I think the number of vampires surprised everyone. People had largely assumed that there just weren't that many in the 'New World.'"

I didn't say anything, though my mind drifted back to the pile of unearthly, inert white bodies in the underground cavern.

Our eyes met briefly, but he looked away quickly. The wipers thumped in time to my heartbeat. "I liked the idea of being a hunter a lot better when I didn't think I'd ever have to actually kill a vampire."

I released the breath I was holding.

"It's hard," he continued, talking almost as if to himself. "You have no idea the amount of hatred I grew up with, and I didn't even realize it. It's hard to shake all the bigotry and the sense of the enemy. But then, here you are."

He looked at me then, and something made my heart thump against my chest.

"I've had a crush on you for so long," he said. "And the first time I finally connect with you, it turns out you're a dhampyr. And it kind of blew my mind, you know? I had to rethink so much."

"Are you going to quit?"

He let out a bitter laugh. "It's not that easy. The hunter mantle is passed down through the generations. I'm an only child. I can't just cast it aside."

"And I'm the princess of the vampires," I said. "I guess we're the lucky ones."

NIKOLAI'S APARTMENT TURNED OUT TO be the top floor of a house in the shadow of the Witch's Hat, a city water tower in the shape of a medieval turret with a conical roof. The affluent, quirky neighborhood was just on the "wrong"—as in Minneapolis—side of the border between the two cities. I admired the caretaker's wild gardening style as Nikolai unlocked the door.

I was surprised to discover we were alone. At my questioning eyebrow, he said, "My roommates have late-afternoon classes."

"Oh," I said, surprised at how small my voice sounded. I'd been alone with guys before, but never one quite so much older. I wondered what he expected. Would he make a move on me? Did I want him to?

The door opened to a secondary interior door and a set of ratty carpet-covered stairs. Nikolai headed up the stairs. They turned at a landing, where someone had hung a life-sized poster of that guy from *Heroes* as Spock. "I liked that movie," I said, trying to make conversation.

"Huh?" Nik gave the poster a glance, and then said, "Oh, that's Stevie's. She's our resident nerd."

She?

Nik used his keys to open the top door. With a flourish, he flung it open. "Welcome to chez Nikolai."

I was impressed.

I'd sort of been expecting the typical bachelor pad, but Nikolai and his roomies had better taste . . . at least upon first impression. The first room was a large window-filled living area. If it had been that sort of day, the place would have been flooded with light. The wraparound couches matched the easy chairs, and they all looked relatively new and stain free. A glass-topped coffee table held an arrangement of dried flowers, but scattered on the top were piles of the latest manga titles and Marvel comics.

Through an archway was a room typically designated as a dining room, but Nik and his friends had clearly declared it the entertainment center. Game consoles, TVs, stereos, and such crammed the walls. What wasn't electronics was bookshelves overflowing with DVDs, CDs, paperback books, more graphic novels and comics, and even someone's vinyl collection. Two doors were visible. One led to a kitchen that seemed piled with pizza boxes and take-out containers, and the other led to a murky hallway and, likely, bedrooms and a bathroom.

"So what do you think?"

"I can't wait to live on my own," I said. "I would love a place like this."

"Let me show you the rest," he said.

I was a little nervous, but he took me by the hand with an excited smile. The darkened hallway did lead to a bathroom, which I glanced at and thought: a lot of boys live here. But after waving in the direction of John and Stevie's room, which I only glimpsed through a beaded curtain, Nik pointed to another set of stairs. "Mike and I get the attic. Wait till you see it. It's awesome."

The attic stairs were narrow and steep, but Nik flicked on a light halfway up that illuminated a wide-open space. The wood plank floors had been finished and polished to a warm glow. The ceiling was high enough for me to stand upright, and full of the exposed beams of a pitched roof. Two skylights had been built into the ceiling. Fresh air poured in from where they were cranked open. Each boy had staked out a dormer with a futon and an arrangement of antique dressers.

It was kind of cool.

And very, very intimate.

I could tell right away which space must be Nikolai's. He had a shiny black and chrome electric guitar propped up by his futon frame. Schoolbooks lay piled on the floor along with papers and a laptop.

Casually, he sat on his bed, and patted a spot for me to sit. I wanted to say I'd prefer to hang out in the living room, but that wasn't entirely true. Gingerly, I took the seat he offered. Our knees touched.

Nik looked especially good today. His longish hair had begun to curl at the ends in the rain, and the T-shirt he wore did little to hide a trim, athletic body. He looked hard, slender, and a little dangerous, like a knife.

A lot about Nikolai reminded me of a weapon, actually. There was something about him, a tautness, that seemed on the verge of going off at any time. It was scary and kind of exciting.

I found myself nervously playing with the hem of my sleeve, wishing I'd worn something a bit less dorky than my ratty old *Sailor Moon* T-shirt and a dowdy raincoat. "So, I listened to your album last night," I admitted. "You're a really good singer."

"Thanks," he said offhandedly. His mind seemed to be on

something else, because his eyes kept drifting away and lighting on various things in the room.

I felt sort of desperate to get his attention, his approval, so I started babbling. "It's not my usual sort of music, mind you, but I thought it was technically, you know, very good. You sound like a very tight band. I really thought that—"

Before I could make a bigger fool out of myself, his mouth stopped mine with a kiss.

Seventeen

ven I know that when you're being kissed by an extremely fine-looking guy, it's not the time to overthink. But my mind, which should have been concentrating on the softness of his lips, jittered. What had brought this on? My oh-so-sexy recounting of his band's attributes? I didn't think so. I'd been my usual dorky, lame self. Had he been thinking about kissing me from the moment he invited me over? Possible—he was a guy after all. Look at how he had maneuvered me out of my rain jacket already, and how his hands slid slowly up the contours of my exposed arms.

Okay, brain gone all melty. No longer thinking.

Instinct took over. My body responded all on its own with no input from me. Despite a nagging sense that this was too fast, I quivered under the heat of his touch. My breath hitched. His hands moved from my arms, and I wanted to whimper and beg him to come back. But the moment they slipped down my sides and under my shirt, my brain snapped back on. Hard.

I pulled away.

"Um," I said, not sure what to say to explain my reaction that wouldn't completely break the moment.

Nikolai had the sense to look chagrined. "I'm sorry," he said. "It's just that I've been thinking about kissing you for so long."

"Really?" I hadn't meant to ask out loud, but it just slipped out. I mean, I'd always thought that he was way more into Bea than me.

He laughed softly. Sitting back until his shoulders rested against the wall, he seemed to be trying to get a good look at me. "Yeah, *really*. I told you I had a crush. Why are you so surprised?"

I rubbed my bare arms, feeling the sudden chill in the absence of our body heat. "I figured you were out of my league." I shrugged. "Anyway, the spooky eye can be kind of a handicap."

Shaking his head, he said, "Are you kidding? That's what makes you so damn hot."

Hot? Me?

The way he looked at me, I knew he was quite serious.

Then he very slowly, cautiously leaned in to give me another peck on the lips.

I let him.

When he lingered there, hopeful, I nudged his mouth open with mine. A little more timidly, he kissed me again. This time I initiated the exploration, and I discovered he tasted good. Not like blood, but still warm and alive.

Hm?

Still, as strange as it was, my heartbeat quickened at that thought. My kiss became more desperate. I wanted to devour him.

A painful stab and a strange clicking sensation warned me to pull away just as my fangs descended.

"Oops," I said, putting my hand in front of my mouth to shield him from my transformation. I mumbled, "My turn to get carried away. Sorry."

He glanced at me from under his lashes and flashed what could only be a come-hither smile. "No need to stop."

Yeah, but now I wanted to *bite* him. How awkward was that?

"Um, I need to . . . uh, go to the bathroom. I'll be right back." And with that, I bolted to the stairs and stumbled down them before he could even utter a word of protest.

Finding the bathroom, I shut the door. I didn't even bother with the light. Nervously, I checked myself in the mirror. Yep. There they were. My canine teeth had elongated and, somehow, sharpened to deadly looking points. At least my eyes hadn't gone all cat-reflect-y.

This was certainly a disturbing development. I couldn't even kiss a boy without wanting to bite him. To say the least, this was going to be hell on my love life. Closing the toilet seat, I sat down dejectedly with my head in my hands. The second my palms hit my cheeks, my damn fangs bit my tongue. "Ow. Goddamn it!"

There was a soft knock at the door. "Are you okay in there?"

"No, this sucks! I bit my own stupid tongue." Okay, I could have edited that to make more sense, but I was startled by his sudden presence and incredibly frustrated by this situation. Did I ask to be a vampire? No. In fact, I hadn't even considered it an option until yesterday. Now everything was fangs, blood, and weird caves. I just wanted to make out a little more with a cool, cute boy.

"Can I help?" Nikolai asked from the other side of the door. Great. Just great. I wiped the well of tears from the corner of my eye. "I mean . . . you can tell me if you think I'm a lousy kisser or whatever."

I whipped open the door, nearly pulling it from the hinges. "No! I like you! I . . ." I faltered because he'd been trying to peer through the keyhole and he stood up suddenly, guiltily.

His eyes were wide and he pointed at my mouth. "Your, um, fangs are showing."

"Oh." My hand flew to cover my mouth. "Oh, crap."

I slammed the door shut. It banged loudly. Awkwardly. My first date with Nikolai was not going at all the way I'd hoped. I could just cry.

"Can we just go bowling? I thought you wanted to bowl," I shouted.

There was a stunned silence from the other side of the door, followed by a chuckle. "Actually, yeah, that sounds like an awesome idea."

ONCE MY FANGS HAD TUCKED themselves away and Nikolai made a few calls to friends, I cautiously let myself out of the bathroom. I was expecting him to act as embarrassed as I felt, but he seemed to have gained a sense of purpose. He offered me my coat at the door and gave me a peck on the cheek. "Let's start over, okay?"

I nodded, grateful for both the suggestion and the kiss. My shoulders dropped the tension I didn't even know I'd been holding. I think I'd been worried he'd want to forgo all the romance and we'd end up just strained friends. I gave him a quick hug. "Thanks," I said. "For understanding."

"I didn't say I wasn't confused." He smiled down at me, our

faces close enough for another kiss. I should have let go, but I didn't want to. "You're very hot and cold, but I can be patient."

"And the fangs?"

I let him out of the hug because I wasn't sure I was going to like this answer as much, but he grasped my hands before I could step away.

"They're weird," he admitted. "A little cute, and very, very naughty."

That confused me. "Naughty?"

"I'm an apprentice fang buster," he said. "Vamps are supposed to be off-limits."

"What about half ones?"

"I guess I'm making an exception."

His eyes were intense and I felt heat rising between us. I hopped up on my tiptoes to peck him on the nose. "Good." I smiled. "Now let's bowl."

BOWLING, IT TURNED OUT, WAS my sport. By the time Nikolai's friends joined us, I had already won two out of three games.

I was raring to take on the new blood, but Nik called for mercy. "Food break," he suggested. "Let's grab some pizza."

The alley that Nikolai had taken me to was Bryant-Lake Bowl. The front half was a swanky Uptown Minneapolis bar/restaurant and the back end was a bowling alley. Apparently, somewhere there was also the entrance to a theater because I saw playbills for upcoming shows all over the walls.

"I'm Stevie," said a tall woman with reddish blond hair, a broad, freckled nose, and an easy smile. I honestly would never have pegged her as the nerd. No horn-rims or braces or poor so-

cial skills there. She wore the uniform of a college student—
T-shirt, jeans, and tennis shoes—but had a relaxed confidence
that instantly put me at ease. "This is my boyfriend, John. Mike
is stuck in Western Civilization."

"Aren't we all?" commented John, who, really, with that joke
seemed much more the geek, though he was clearly trying for in-
tellectual chic. He had round Harry Potter glasses and a thin
face dotted with stubble.

Nikolai introduced me by my full first name, which he said
with a surprising grace, though he added his own Romany ac-
cent. I smiled at the sound of it on his lips, but added, "Just call
me Ana. It's easier."

"No, no, Anastasija is lovely," John insisted. "It's regal."

"You're thinking of the Romanovs," Stevie said. "Maybe Ana
doesn't appreciate the association. I mean, things ended badly
for them."

While the two of them argued over my name, Nikolai found
a table large enough to accommodate the four of us. Before we
even settled, a waitress deposited menus and glasses of water.
She hurried off to the next table before I could even thank her.

"Are you Russian like Nikolai?" John asked.

No, I thought, vampire. Instead, I just shook my head. "English, I think."

"Ah, then we're bitter enemies," John said with a smile. Hooking a thumb at his chest, he said, "Irish."

"And I'm half French and part Finnish and some Bulgarian,"
Stevie said with a roll of her eyes, and a hearty laugh. "Are we
done with the ethnic identification? I'm starving!"

"Be serious," John muttered. "You're not Bulgarian."

"Says who?" She poked him in the ribs.

"Are they always like this?" I asked Nikolai.

He nodded. "Pretty much, except when they're having sex. Then they argue louder."

"Nice," Stevie said, but she was smiling.

Meanwhile, I was glad the restaurant had muted lighting. It hid my blush.

My phone rang. It was Mom. Everyone was watching me, so I stood up to excuse myself. "I'd better take this," I said.

As I put the phone to my ear, I expected the worst. Instead, she said, "Are you okay?"

The question stunned me, as did my reaction. "It's been a weird day," I admitted, surprising myself by wanting to hear her reassuring tone. The bar was noisy. I moved toward the bowling alley in my slippery-soled shoes. I sat down on one of the plastic swivel seats near an empty lane. "I licked this guy at school I don't even really like, although now everyone thinks I do. I ran out of school. Then Elias came and we ended up underground, and now I'm bowling."

I left out the part where Nikolai and I made out, because, well, I thought she might have a heart attack as it was.

"When are you coming home?"

That was it? No yelling?

"What have you done with my mother?" I asked the alien on the phone.

"I'm just glad you're safe," Mom said, and she sounded sincere. I cradled the phone to my ear. "I got the automated notice about your truancy on the machine. I called Helena to find out what Bea knew, and she just said there was an accident in gym class."

"Thompson got hit in the face with a hockey puck."

"But you're okay?"

"No, Mom, not really," I said.

"What's wrong, honey?"

I looked over where Nikolai and his friends sat. They were laughing about something and Stevie jabbed poor John in the ribs again. That guy must have a constant bruise in that spot.

"I'm out with Nikolai," I said in lieu of answering. I wanted to spill everything again, in greater detail, but Mom was a witch. She hated vampires. She wasn't going to tell me it would all be okay, like I desperately wanted her to, even if she was acting conciliatory. "He asked me out bowling with some of his friends."

"Nikolai Kirov? From the coven?"

I could hear the smile in her tone. I knew she'd approve. She'd wanted me to hook up with a witch boy since middle school. Most of the time I found it deeply embarrassing; it was nice to finally use it to my advantage. "Yeah, he gave me a ride home last night and we really hit it off."

"Do be careful," she started, and I rolled my eyes in anticipation of the "safe sex" lecture. Instead, she said, "His family hunts vampires."

By chance, I glanced over at Nik at the very instant he looked for me. Our eyes met. "No," I told her. "He said he's making an exception."

There was silence on the other end for a moment. "You should come home. It's a school night."

I checked the wall clock; it wasn't even dinnertime. And anyway, I still wasn't sure I was going home, plus I'd promised Elias I'd show up for the debut thingie, so I said, "I love you. Got to run. Good-bye!"

I had the phone clicked shut and shoved into my pocket

before she even said good-bye. I didn't want a fight to ruin everything. My face must have betrayed something when I got to the table because Nik asked, "Everything okay?" He stood up to let me back into the seat nearest the window.

"Yeah. Just my mom checking in," I explained.

"We ordered appetizers. I hope that's okay," Stevie said.

"You eat meat, don't you?" John asked.

"Yeah, I do," I said, wedging myself back into my seat. Everyone had a drink of some kind. From what I could tell, everyone was having pop. I pointed at my glass and looked at Nikolai.

"I got you a Coke. Regular. I hope that's okay?"

I smiled. Ah, normal. Friends out for the evening. No one talking about Initiations or vampires. Just what I needed. I let their conversation about their professors and blue books drift around me. Nikolai reached out and held my hand under the table. I gave him a gentle squeeze. This was great.

Which was why I nearly jumped out of my bowling shoes when I saw Elias watching me from across the room.

Eighteen

Okay, new question. Elias Constantine: (a) dashing vampire protector or (b) creepy stalker guy?

What would have been an easy "a" ten minutes ago now had me wondering. Maybe it was the way the light caught his unblinking, steady gaze that seemed to bore right through me, or the fact that I was hyperaware that I held Nikolai's hand under the table.

But something about Elias's presence in the darkened bar made me swallow nervously.

Trust the other girl at the table to notice my distraction. Stevie swiveled to try to see who'd caught my eye. As the boys continued to discuss the merits of retaking a failed thermal-physics class, she leaned in conspiratorially. "You look like you've seen a ghost."

No, I wanted to say, a vampire.

But when I started to point to where Elias had been sitting a second ago, he was gone. "That's weird," I said, scanning the bar to try to spot where he went. But I saw no sign of him. "He was there a minute ago."

"Who?" Nikolai asked.

"That's what I was trying to find out," Stevie chided.

"Some guy I met the other night," I said distractedly. Had he slipped off to the bathroom? Where did Elias go?

"The other night?" Nikolai asked anxiously. "You mean, like, *last* night?"

"Did something happen last night?" Stevie asked.

Even John was paying more attention. "At the Gypsy dance class?" he asked. "Are you guys in that together?"

Gypsy dance class? Was that where Nikolai had told his friends he was going last night dressed for the Initiation? I tried to catch his eye to give him silent grief about it, but his head craned this way and that, searching the crowded bar. His body was tense, as if on full alert.

He knew.

Nikolai sensed a vampire was here.

"It's okay," I said, grabbing for the hand Nikolai had released the moment I mentioned seeing someone. "He's a friend."

The eyes that met mine were full of fury. "Of yours maybe, but not mine."

"But I thought . . ."

He stood up. Nikolai's entire posture was full of challenge.

I put a restraining hand on Nikolai. The moment we touched, I felt his magic. His whole body surged with power. It jangled along his nerves, bright and sharp. Where his hand clenched into a fist, I sensed a focal point almost like the tip of a blade. If I squinted, I could see the outline of a shimmering purple point emanating from his knuckles, as though he held a knife between his fingers.

"He's gone," I said, trying to tug Nik back into his seat.

"Yeah, no need to go all alpha male," Stevie teased.

I tried to muster a smile to show her that everything was okay, but Nikolai remained on full alert.

"What's going on?" John asked.

Nikolai bolted for the door. Outside the window, I caught sight of Elias standing in the shadow of an alleyway across the street.

"Wait," I shouted, running after him, skating on the floor in my bowling shoes.

"This is not your fight," he told me when I reached him just outside the door. Smokers milled around us. Embers flared and danced in the misty darkness. "Go back inside where it's safe. This isn't just any vampire. He's a captain in their army, a Praetorian Guard."

"Elias?"

Nikolai's attention suddenly focused hotly on me. He pulled me away from the door and under the awning. His amber eyes flashed threateningly. "You have a name? A full name? Give it to me!"

No way.

I might not have passed the Initiation, but I knew names had power. "I can't," I told him. "It's like I told you; he's my friend."

Nikolai's face twisted. His eyes narrowed. The hand on my arm clenched tighter, more painfully, and I could feel his magic ramping up even higher. Would he use it against me?

I didn't have time to consider what I might do if Nikolai did, because, in an instant, Elias was at my side. With a great shove, he pushed himself between Nikolai and me.

"Unhand her." Elias's voice was a low growl.

I felt kind of stupid and useless, pressed between the window of the bar and Elias's back. The smokers began reacting to the altercation. Someone demanded to know what was going on. "Hey!" another shouted.

Nikolai, who'd seemed ready to impale Elias with the blade of his magic, lowered his arm slowly. "Consider yourself lucky, sucker," Nikolai said. "Or should I say 'Elias'?"

Elias stiffened at that, but didn't back down. "Say what you wish, Nikolai Kirov; you are not a hunter yet."

I peeked around Elias's shoulder just in time to see Nikolai take a step forward. He poked Elias in the chest, and I sensed the sharpness of the magical jab that made Elias stumble back, nearly crushing me against the window. "All I have to do is make my first kill."

"If you dare, pup," Elias said, pulling himself upright. "But I'll make you a solemn promise as well. Bring harm to my lady and it will be your death knell ringing."

Before they could go into another round of "oh, yeah's," the door sprang open and Stevie and John came flooding out into the night. "Are you guys okay? What's going on?"

I felt a soft breeze, like a chaste kiss on my cheek. I knew Elias was gone, disappeared into the night.

WE WENT BACK INSIDE TO strained silence. Stevie figured out that Nikolai and I needed to talk, so she told John she needed his help fetching some appetizers. He protested that the waitress could do that until she poked him in the ribs again and he got it. They excused themselves and left Nik and me together.

I knew I should make good use of the time Stevie bought me,

but I just sat staring at him. His whole body was shaking from the exchange. He couldn't look at me, but all I could do was gape. Despite what he'd said to me, Nikolai seemed ready to stake Elias. I felt deeply betrayed.

"Are you okay?" he asked me. "Man, that was close."

I frowned in confusion. He thought *I'd* been in danger? "Elias was protecting me from you, Nik."

"Your Elias is a butcher, Ana. He's a ruthless killer. I may only know him by reputation, but his reputation is infamous."

"I thought I'd changed your mind about vampires."

Nik folded the corners of the paper napkin under his empty, sweat-streaked glass. "I don't want to hurt *you*," he said to the table. Then he looked up at me. "I never want to hurt you. But I'm honor-bound by blood."

"I am so damn sick of blood," I said, cutting him off. "Why? Why do you have to have this stupid duty to the family you were born into? Why can't you just be your own self and follow your own heart?"

"What does your heart tell you, Ana? Are you a vampire or a witch?"

I didn't have a good answer for that, and anyway, Stevie and John came back to the table, after having retrieved a plate of nachos with cheese and all the trimmings. With the presence of food, our conversation stopped.

The rest of the meal I spent stealing glances out the window, hoping to catch sight of Elias. Meanwhile, Nikolai lied smoothly to his friends about the whole dustup, claiming Elias was some old boyfriend of mine he was jealous of. I didn't object. In fact, I didn't say much of anything.

I was still mulling over my answer to Nikolai's question. It seemed obvious that I couldn't delay the decision much longer. What was I? Was I one of Elias's people or Nik's?

I wasn't entirely sure I liked either choice.

And did I have to choose between Nik and Elias? If I had to, which would I pick?

The physical attraction between Nikolai and me was hard to deny. I liked kissing him—no doubt. But this hunter part of him I wasn't so sure about. He talked about making a kill. He threatened Elias.

What kept coming back to me? Elias's response. It wasn't, "Oh yeah, well, I'll kill you first." No, Elias made it clear that if Nikolai hurt *me*, he'd have trouble on his hands.

It made me really consider everything I'd learned about vampires so far. There was a lot of talk from Nikolai about how horrible they were; they drank blood—Elias even admitted that they did—but . . . ruthless killers? I was having trouble buying that. I tried to think about all the "missing persons" reports I'd read in the newspapers or heard of through the grapevine at school and in the coven. I tried to remember the last unsolved murder I'd heard of. Frankly, there weren't a lot. If vampires were systematically feeding on us, you'd think the coven, at least, would be talking about it.

You'd think there'd be a whole bunch of "stay safe" rules regarding getting drained dry by the local band of vampires.

Of which there were quite a few.

I'd seen their lair.

That was a lot of vampire to "feed." They'd make quite a dent in the population of St. Paul if they were noshing on us on a regular basis. Maybe they went over to Minneapolis to hunt, but you'd still think this area would be the murder capital of the world if all those vampires were killing to eat.

Elias had said the hunt was nothing to fear. Nikolai even agreed that vampires had a lot of rituals around their blood drinking.

So they couldn't be mass murderers. There was just no way it was practical.

Nikolai, on the other hand, clearly said he had to make a "kill" before he could become a full vampire hunter.

I looked over at Nik, who was talking animatedly to Stevie about some science fiction television show on cable I never watched. It was hard to imagine that those hands, which had so gently caressed my skin, were capable of violence.

Yet, he'd threatened to kill Elias.

What was I doing with this guy? And what should I do now? I wanted to get out of here, but I didn't know where to go.

I excused myself from the table, claiming a need to visit the toilet. I made my way to the bathroom and found a quiet spot nearby with halfway decent cell reception. I looked at the bars. I could call home. Mom and I had an agreement. She trusted me to go out with friends as long as I promised to call for a ride if I felt unsafe for any reason.

But if I called her and bailed, I'd never be able to date Nikolai again. I mean, maybe I was exaggerating this whole killer thing, and then how stupid would I look if I ran out on our first date by calling my mom? How would I explain that? Plus, what about Mom? Was she still ready to put the hex on me to keep me under lock and key? I'd been ready to be homeless tonight. Which was the fire and which was the frying pan?

I considered other options. There was the city bus. Taylor's dad drove a taxi. Bea had a car.

No, strike that last one. I couldn't call Bea. I was persona non grata with her, and I'd sent her that kind of snotty text. I hadn't checked her response, but I could guess what it was.

It was Taylor's dad, the city bus, or my mom. I was ready to eenie-meanie-mynie-mo it when Nikolai came up to stand beside me. I'd been leaning against the wall between the bowling alley and the door to the ladies'.

"Busy?" He jerked his chin in the direction of the bathroom.

I gave him a long, serious look. "No. I was thinking about how you scared me and trying to decide whether I should get a ride home from somebody else."

He laughed lightly. "I do love that honesty."

"Do you? Well, then, how's this for you? I'm beginning to think witches might be way worse than vampires. There's a lot of talk about how they're so evil. But so far I haven't seen it. In fact, you seem like the aggressive one. Do they really come after you—or any of us?"

Nikolai's eyes snapped angrily. I felt his power flare momentarily. Then with a breath, he consciously let it go. "It might seem like that, but you've been purposely kept in the dark. And this is America. The New World has fewer vampires, less history. But the short answer? Yes. Yes, they come after us. They come after us in packs. And when they catch us? It isn't pretty."

I frowned. I had firsthand experience with fangs. I was sure vampires could be formidable enemies. But I wasn't quite ready to let go of my theory that maybe we were the aggressors in this little war. "So we kill them to defend ourselves."

Nikolai nodded.

"How come I don't hear about the vampires' attacks?"

"Because. Thanks to the vigilance of the hunters, there hasn't been an organized strike in centuries."

Centuries? Did that sound a bit like circular logic? They're horrible because they kill us, so we kill them to keep them from killing us.

Still, what did I know about it? Nik was right. I'd been consciously kept out of this discussion, while his family was smack in the middle of it. "Okay," I quietly acquiesced, though I wasn't sold at all.

"Do you want me to take you home now?"

His eyes watched mine for a sign. I could tell he was hopeful that I hadn't completely gone off him.

I hadn't, had I?

"Can we go somewhere, just the two of us, and talk?" I asked.

He smiled warmly, with just a hint of something more feral. "I'd like that."

AFTER TURNING IN OUR SHOES and saying good-bye to Stevie and John, Nikolai and I made our way farther into Uptown. He parked near Lake Calhoun. Though the air still held a touch of dampness, it had warmed considerably. I still had my raincoat, so I agreed to his offer of a stroll around the park.

"What about vampires? Aren't you worried they're going to jump out at us if we talk about them too loudly?" I asked as we made our way down a narrow set of stairs to the broad walkway. I could hear the waves lap quietly against the shore, but the lake was little more than a broad expanse of dark. Electric lights glittered distantly on the far side.

"I'll protect you," he said.

A nice offer, but I didn't really expect that Elias would attack me, after all. What I didn't want was another skirmish. I didn't want either of them to get hurt. Or any other vamp for that matter.

My eyes searched the shadows. Knowing that Elias would be near, I only hoped he had sense enough to stay hidden.

The moon, only barely past its fullness, rose round and yellow over the beech trees. The shore smelled faintly of rotting fish, but the city noise seemed to fade a little in the tall shadows of the sailboats at dock.

"It's been a crazy start for us, huh?" Nikolai asked softly.

He took my hand in his. It was meant to be a romantic gesture, I imagine, except he must have forgotten about the residue from the magical knife he'd almost used on Elias. A painful zing, like a jolt of electricity, shot up my arm.

"Ouch!" I said, flapping my hand, trying to get the feeling back.

Nikolai looked at his palm. He glanced at me. "What happened there?"

"It must be leftover zap from the blade."

"Still?" He seemed to be peering at me where we stopped near the beach house. "You must be very sensitive. Most witches don't even see it, much less feel it."

"I'm not most witches, am I? In fact, technically, I'm not a witch at all anymore."

There was a short pier stretching out into the water. I walked out to the end and leaned against the railing. The water was silent and dark. Gnats batted against the tall light overhead.

Nikolai came up beside me and carefully put his *other* hand on my shoulder. His body was warm, comforting. I leaned into it. "I don't buy it, you know," Nikolai said. "You're a witch too."

I squinted at him and made a face. "You were there. You saw me fail. It was a disaster."

"You didn't pass the Initiation. Big deal."

It was to me, but I didn't say anything.

"There's more than one way to be a witch. My mother's people don't have any kind of special initiation. They just *are*. Her people respect magic for what it is because they have a lot of power without robes or words or flash. It's power, like yours. Sensitivity."

I thought about that while he held me close. We listened to the slap of the water against the dock. Nikolai's family wasn't part of the big Book of Shadows either. The coven had accepted him as an insider, though, because his magic was demonstrable. He was the first in his family to be a True Witch. His name would be added.

"Why did you want to be a True Witch?" I asked him. "Why not just practice Romany magic, like your mother?"

In the harsh light, Nikolai's face darkened. I saw the muscle of his jaw flex as he considered his answer. "A True Witch is a better hunter. Magic can bind vampires."

It all came back to being a hunter for him. I hid my discomfort by peeling paint from the rail with my fingernail.

Nikolai continued. "When it was clear I had magical potential, my father insisted we find a mentor for me, someone to make introductions. My mother knew of True Witches, of course. Her Romany blood helped open doors."

"What about your dad? Is he a witch too? I thought only magic could trap and kill a vampire."

"Like I said, there are all sorts of magic and magicians. Vampire hunters have very specific spells, but it was seen as an advantage to have the magic of a True Witch as well."

"And now you're one," I said.

"Yeah," he said looking out over the lake. "I know this probably sounds like a cop-out, but I have been trained to kill vampires my whole life. When I see one, instinct takes over. There's no thinking involved, only action."

"And if you saw my fangs, would you just act?"

He didn't answer right away, but then, quietly, he said, "I hope to hell not."

"Me too," I said.

I shifted slightly under his arm, but he didn't let go easily. Instead, he gave my shoulders a hug before releasing me. "I don't want to lie to you," he said. "I know this isn't going to be easy for us, for me. I know you wish I could just abandon everything I am, but even if I could, I'm not sure I want to. I still believe in my cause. Vampires are much darker than I think you know. I can't walk away from my duty to my family, my coven, and, frankly, humanity."

Humanity's end, that's what Elias had called his people. But he was talking about a part of me. "What if I became one of them? Would you be duty-bound to stop me?"

He didn't break our gaze. "Maybe."

Well, it was honest. "You believe that strongly that vampires are evil?"

"I do," he said, though his conviction sounded heavy on him. It seemed to me that he carried quite a burden. I found it noble, and not unlike Elias's knightly duties. In their own ways, they were soldiers on opposite sides of an ancient war.

I kissed him. It was tentative. After all, I was still so very confused about how I felt about him. He scared me. He excited me. His violence disturbed me, but his compassion touched me. I could sympathize about the family pressure and the weight of his duty.

He wasn't an easy choice; that was for sure.

We kissed for a while, just a cautious exploration. It was nice, until the mosquitoes found us and started biting. With a laugh, we dashed back to the car, arms wrapped around each other's waist.

I didn't want to go home, but it seemed the thing to do. Nikolai sensed my reluctance, and we meandered along the side streets when the highway would have had me home in minutes.

"Maybe we could do this again sometime," Nikolai suggested when we finally parked in front of my house. We'd driven past it three times, thanks to the wards. "You know, my band is having a release party. I could get you in, if you want to come."

According to Taylor, it was only the hottest ticket in town. I thought about acting cool, but it really wasn't my style. "Are you kidding? That would be awesome!"

And the first ever band party of my life!

"When is it?" I asked, trying not to bounce like a giddy schoolgirl.

"Tomorrow night."

"Count me in!"

"Good. I can finally tell the guys I'm bringing a girlfriend. They've been teasing me that I'm gay. I just told them the right one hadn't come along. Until now, that is."

Was he trying to melt my heart? This time his kiss was sweet and lingering. It was hard to say good-bye.

*   *   *

I EXPECTED MOM TO BE waiting up for me, but Dad?

"Where have you been?" his voice boomed out of the mulberry thicket at the side of the porch.

I totally felt busted, so I responded sheepishly. "Uh, out?"

"Do you know what time it is?"

Wait a minute, I thought. This was ridiculous. This guy might be biologically my dad, but he wasn't a parent. Moreover, he was crouched barefoot under the window between the mulberry trees and the juniper bush like some crazed Peeping Tom. "What's it to you?"

He stepped out of the bushes. I'm sure it was meant to be dramatic and regal, but the juniper grew thickly and he had to wiggle his way out awkwardly. Needles rained on his toes. "Anastasija, we had hoped for your debut."

Oh, yeah, right. I'd forgotten about that. "Elias is supposed to escort me."

My father nodded approvingly. "Excellent. We shall meet him at the gate."

APPARENTLY DAD KNEW THE COOL way into the underground. No going down a sewer drain for the prince of vampires. I was only a little unnerved to discover how close the entrance was to my house.

We walked a few blocks to the point where the slope of Crocus Hill began to descend. The evening breeze caught a few rusty brown oak leaves and they drifted to the ground. Crickets chirped slower, as if forlorn, in the colder air.

"Here," he said as we approached a park, empty and abandoned in the faded light. The brick recreation-center building made a stark silhouette against the starry sky. A sidewalk ran parallel to a short strip of grass. Beyond stood a row of trees and a wild tangle of weeds, and, I knew from experience, a steep cliff.

Dad, of course, headed straight to the edge.

"I'm glad you're a sensible girl," he said, reaching out to take my hand to steady me as he led me over a short, orange fence meant to keep people like us from tumbling over the cliff unaware. "Jeans and tennis shoes are good for this kind of hike. Not like the frivolities of the court. Though I'd have had you wear a warmer jacket on such a chilly night."

I snorted, and resisted the urge to sigh "Dad" at him. As we picked our way through the burrs that kept snagging at the calves of my pants, I asked, "Can you see? I mean, better than I can, which, by the way, is almost not at all?"

It was true. Once we were away from the soft glow of the streetlamps, the darkness grew almost as thick as the tall grasses. Mosquitoes buzzed my ears, and every step disturbed hordes of leaping grasshoppers. I was starting to feel very creepy-crawly.

"Watch your footing," he cautioned, as he started down.

As if on cue, I slid on the crumbly, hard-packed dirt, and landed on my butt. "How can you see anything?"

"Relax. Breathe," he said, sounding like a yoga coach. "You can see if you allow yourself to."

Still sitting on the hard-packed dirt, I stared up at him. Then I sighed. I might as well try, even though it sounded very Jedi woo-woo to me. I closed my eyes for a moment, and took a deep breath and used the relaxation techniques I learned from my witch Elders. I let my shoulders drop, and focused on just taking in air and releasing it. I opened my eyes again.

It was still dark, but everything had a silvery sheen to it. I could clearly see the outlines of the hillside, the trees, and even the soccer field below. I blinked rapidly, disbelieving. "How did that work?"

My dad, looking all funky with a silvery halo around his body, smiled. "You're my daughter. Darkness cannot be your enemy." Then he pointed just beyond a cluster of maple trees. "We're almost to the cave. Let's go."

The steepness of the hill made it awkward for me to stand, but I managed to do it without sliding farther down. I did have to grab on to tufts of grass to haul myself up to where my dad waited, all graceful. "When am I going to get the rest of the woodland-elf powers?"

"When you allow yourself to," he said as if that explained everything. Threading his way easily through the maples, he pointed to an indentation in the side of the hill. It looked more like a deer's hollow than a cave's entrance. He waited for me to catch up to him.

The fecund scent of moist earth grew stronger as we approached the entrance. Absently, I wiped my palms against the material of my jeans. I wasn't looking forward to another blind grope through a dirt tunnel, especially after today's rain. The place would be all mud. And worms. Uck. Just as I considered a good excuse to skip my debut, Elias emerged from the mouth of the cave, like a sultan stepping out from a silken tent.

"My prince." He looked a little surprised to find us there as he bowed deeply. "Princess."

Dad chuckled. "My dear captain, I hear you are to be my daughter's companion for the evening."

Elias kept his eyes lowered, and his head tilted downward slightly. "Only if you allow it, Highness."

For some reason this made Dad laugh louder. "I suspect if I forbade anything, my daughter would want it even more."

I was kind of offended by the implication, especially since Dad hardly knew me, but since it was mostly true, all I could think to say was, "Dad!"

Elias just stood there not knowing what to do either. It was strange to see him so baffled and embarrassed. He seemed like the sort of guy who always knew what to do in any situation. Watching him now, the way he seemed to bounce ever so slightly on the balls of his feet, I could tell he was less of a courtier and more of a man of action, a soldier.

Dad's grin grew wider with each passing moment. "Come, come," he said finally. "Offer your arm already, man. We have a party to attend."

To MY SURPRISE AND GREAT relief, we didn't enter the cave. Instead, my father continued to lead us through the woods. More than once I was grateful that my arm was slipped into the crook of Elias's arm, when the weeds tripped me or an uneven patch of ground threatened to knock me on my ass again. We must have made a very strange procession, strolling like lords and ladies through the undergrowth.

"How are you this evening?" Elias asked politely. "I see you've misplaced—erm, abandoned?—your previous escort."

I snorted. "You mean Nikolai? I didn't abandon him. I'm going to see him tomorrow, in fact."

"Oh really?" With my weird silvery vision, I could see the quirk of Elias's eyebrow. "I wonder what he will make of you after tonight."

I stopped walking to stare at him. "What does that mean?"

"If successful, this evening should be quite transformative," Elias said cryptically. He shared a concerned glance with Dad.

I had to carefully parse Elias's sentence. Transformative? I was going to change in some way? It was my turn to look to Dad. "Is this true? What kind of ceremony is this, exactly?"

He nodded. "I thought you knew. I thought perhaps Elias explained this already." Beside me, Elias dropped his head as if in admission of negligence. Dad sighed lightly, then continued. "This ceremony is on par with the Wiccaning. In fact, it's the reason I didn't want you to go through with the other ceremony. You can be witch or demon. Tonight you will become one of us."

"Oh."

Before I could say anything else, Elias put a warm hand over mine where it curled, unfeeling, in the hollow of his arm. "Is this not what you wish, Highness?"

My dad was shaking his head. "She's already tasted first blood. It hardly matters what she wants."

A motorcycle's engine whined down a nearby street. It seemed unreal and distant in the stand of woods.

Elias shifted, as if stiffening uncomfortably. "Respectfully, Highness, I disagree. The applicant must be a willing participant."

"We cannot afford to wait," Dad said, his tone clipped. "The witches will make their next move soon, no doubt to bring her in closer. She's still under their protection."

"And their hunter's son courts her," Elias mumbled.

I nearly kicked him in the shins, but instead I pulled my hand from his arm forcefully. "It's not like that," I said to the angry flash in Dad's eyes. "Nik's had a crush on me for a while, like, for two years or something. He said he's not using me for any of this political stuff. I believe him."

"Naive girl," Dad snarled, fangs flashing in the moonlight.

Elias raised his hands for peace. "This isn't what's important right now. The boy's intentions can be argued at another time, my prince. We should hasten to the debut. The court will be waiting."

Dad calmed visibly as Elias spoke. Then he released the last of his tension with a shrug. "As usual you speak sensibly, Constantine."

Elias put his hand to his heart and bowed his head in acknowledgment. To me, he offered his arm. I hesitated. Was this what I wanted, to be a full vampire? To turn my back on my witch heritage . . . my humanity?

"Perhaps I can assuage some of my lady's fears if I explain the debut more fully as we walk?"

Okay, I could agree to that. Hesitantly, I tucked my hand back under his arm. "All right."

"First, your father will take up a position of honor. Then I will announce your name and title to the court. You will curtsy to your father as a sign of respect."

I nodded. This all sounded pretty normal so far. We'd been walking so long that I was beginning to wonder where we were. I could still hear city sounds—the occasional hiss of a passing car or an airplane overhead—but I'd completely lost my sense of direction. The hill had mostly evened out, and I thought I could smell the river. I felt for sure we should have hit a row of houses or come into downtown by now.

Instead, we came to a clearing, an open park, really. I could see that people had gathered on the basketball court. They held candles, and seemed to be dressed for prom, or a cocktail party. Sequins glittered in the candlelight. The men wore everything from tuxes to kilts to Middle Eastern–looking robes.

I should have worn my sundress, damn it!

Someone had a fiddle, and was playing a light air. I was about to tell Elias how beautiful it all looked when he continued: "And then a sacred hunt will begin."

"Wait," I said, thinking I didn't much like the sound of "hunt." It could be very, um, bloody. "Uh, what?"

"You'll do fine," my dad said with a light little pat on my back, like we were talking about midterms or something completely benign. Then, he bounded down the hill to join the gathering.

"Hunt?" I looked at Elias, my hands on my hips. "I'm not going down there until you explain exactly what that is."

"It's nothing to worry about," he said, but I noticed he didn't meet my eyes when he said it. Instead, he stared darkly down at where my father moved through the throng, shaking hands like a politician.

"I thought I already satisfied the requirements of the hunt when that whole thing with Thompson happened," I said.

Elias glanced sidelong at me for a moment, his mouth a grim line. "First blood, technically—the first of the hunts. Think of it as baptism. This one will be confirmation."

"Baptism? Confirmation, are you serious?" I shook my head at him. "And you wonder why people think you're demons?"

He sniffed as if to say he didn't want to talk about it, his attention still on my dad's meanderings through the crowd.

I sat down in the grass and started picking sticky burrs from where they were stuck on the hems of my jeans in huge brown clumps.

Elias gave me an irritated glance. "We should go. The ceremony will start soon."

"I told you I'm not going anywhere until you explain this thing to me," I said. Then catching his glance, I added emphatically, "Fully."

It was obvious from his posture, all crossed arms and frowns, that he didn't want to tell me. "It's called"—he let out a sigh—"the kill hunt."

"What?!" I jumped to my feet, burrs still clinging to my fingertips. "It's called the what??"

"Calm down," he said, since I was already backing away, ready to bolt for home. He rubbed his face, like he'd suspected I'd react like this but that it still gave him a headache. "It's representational magic. Mostly."

"'Mostly' isn't convincing me much," I all but shouted.

He put his hands up. "Okay, okay. I know you can understand this; you've had training in magic. We're going to—all of us—go into an altered state."

He seemed to be fumbling, so I offered, "Like a trance?"

"Yes," he said, clearly pleased that I seemed to be following along and hadn't entirely bolted.

It didn't mean I liked what he was suggesting, but I gave him an encouraging nod anyway. "Okay, so everyone is going to go into some kind of trance? How?"

"The punch is spiked with blood," he said, with a bit of a squint, like he expected this news to freak me out more. When I didn't react with anything stronger than raised eyebrows, he continued. "You'll be encouraged to drink more and more. The music will get faster; drumbeats will speed up."

I could see it all pretty well. We never did anything quite like this in the coven, but it wasn't unheard of as a way to achieve certain religious experiences.

"When everything reaches a crescendo, the pack will begin to run," he said. His eyes left mine again, and he quietly added, "Until we reach the offering, where we'll feast."

"The offering sounds pretty ominous, Elias. What aren't you saying?"

He smiled lightly, like he appreciated that I called him on it. "I can't pull anything over on you, can I?"

"Yeah, so quit dodging."

"The offering is exactly what you're thinking it is," he said.

"Human." I shuddered.

"Most of the time the offering survives the ordeal, no worse for the wear. It's a risk, though, that the volunteer fully understands when he or she agrees to participate." He sounded as though he was trying to convince himself, especially since I noticed he'd gone back to anxiously watching the people below. "Ultimately, it will be your choice how far things go. The court follows your lead tonight."

"But I'm going to be totally stoned on blood," I pointed out, remembering how intoxicated that tiny taste of Thompson had made me. "What if I accidentally go too far?"

"You won't," he said. "It is my experience, my lady, that the hunt brings out the true nature of the demon it possesses."

"So what about your hunt? Did you kill?"

He stared into my eyes a bit too long and a bit too intensely before he said, "I'm not you, Princess."

I'm so not comforted by what you're implying, I thought but didn't dare voice. "Uh-huh," was what I managed instead.

I managed not to shrink away when Elias came over and put a hand lightly on my shoulder. "I'm overdue," he said, indicating the party below. "I will announce you in a few minutes, once everything is prepared. It's going to be okay. I know you. You're a good person. Trust yourself and your instincts and everything will be fine."

"Okay," I agreed hollowly.

He surprised me by leaning down and lightly kissing my lips tenderly. The affection was unmistakable, and my breath left my lungs in response. I blinked up at him, and he smoothed my hair away from my forehead.

"I'm looking forward to being under your spell," he said. "I suspect your hunt will be like no other."

"No pressure," I joked weakly.

He continued to stroke my hair. "The court needs your influence, my princess. We've lost our . . . humanity. When you're a full vampire, you will change us, become a part of our consciousness. You're exactly what we need."

He kissed me again, still chastely, but with so much emotion, it brought a blush to my cheek.

"Uh, thanks," I murmured.

He released my hair, and stepped away. I felt his absence physically, as the cold air seemed to rush in place of his heat. He waved a quick good-bye before hurrying to join his prince and his people.

Lamely, I lifted a few fingers in a farewell. He turned around to give me a reassuring smile, but it didn't work. The night felt oppressively dark. I clung to the scrawny trunk of a scrub tree. Through the tangle of branches, the vampire ball glittered. When it occurred to me that they were literally "dressed to kill," a bubble of hysterical laughter almost surfaced in my throat.

At that moment, I knew I couldn't go through with it. I wasn't nearly as awesome as Elias seemed to think I was. And I couldn't take the risk. What if I couldn't stop? What if the bloodlust was too much for me to handle? I couldn't be responsible for someone's death, volunteer or not. I really wouldn't be human anymore if that happened.

How could I be?

How could I even live with myself?

Something seemed to change below. The party quieted expectantly. My heart thudded in my chest. I had to get out of there, fast.

And then, before Elias could come for me, I turned and headed for home.

WAS IT TOO MUCH TO ask after that bizarre scene for Mom to be sound asleep on the couch, snuggled under the green fuzzy blanket with a book propped up on her knees and her glasses pushed up into her curls?

I hesitantly peeped in that direction. Could it be true? A snore confirmed it! Fate finally smiled on me.

As quietly as I could, I shut the door and set my backpack

down. I slipped off my shoes and slid on stocking feet to the stairs.

The ancient floorboards betrayed me. The first step creaked and moaned.

"Ana?"

"Mom. Hey. I thought you were asleep."

Mom checked her watch. "It's after midnight."

"And I'm back from the ball!" I tried to make a Cinderella joke, but Mom was unimpressed.

Her frown deepened, and she put her glasses on straight. Standing up, she started methodically folding the blanket. Never a good sign, by the way. "We need to finally have that talk," she said. "About your father and about vampires."

Mom made hot chocolate, and we took our customary spots around the dining room table. I wanted to point out that this was the very scene of the debacle that was the whole "birds and bees" discussion, but I kept my mouth shut. I really wanted to hear what Mom had to say about vampires.

She folded and unfolded her hands and seemed to be trying out different openers in her mind. Finally, she said, "I married your father to end a war."

The hot cocoa in my mouth nearly ended up all over my shirt. "You were married?"

"Technically, we still are. It's, um, that you needed to be legitimate in every way. We were handfasted and married in a . . . in the manner of your father's people."

"What was that like?" I mean, I couldn't picture it. Did Mom actually go down into their underground cavern? Or did they stand naked in a park? She never wore a ring. What did vampires exchange for vows?

Mom actually smiled a bit at the memory. "It was . . . unique."

"Are there pictures?"

"No, thank the Goddess," she said, taking a sip from her University of Minnesota mug. "I was young and at the time I thought the treaty would really work. I truly believed there was more in common with our races than not. And your father . . . he was so handsome, so noble."

I nodded. "Noble" was a good word to describe the vampires I'd met so far. Except for the whole killing people as part of the hunting ritual, that is. My stomach twisted at the thought.

Mom watched me carefully. She shook her head. "They're not, Ana. They're demons direct from hell."

"I thought they were older than all that."

Mom's eyebrow arched. "I see you've been talking to them." I didn't respond to that accusation one way or the other. Eventually, she continued. "It's true, but consider this important fact. All the stories of devils and demons are based on our friends out there. They're full of darkness and evil, and they will corrupt you."

Okay, now my mother had been replaced by some wacko fundamentalist. "Corrupt me? Are you being serious?"

"Yes," she said. Her hands roamed over the coffee cup, as if searching for some answer there. Her eyes darted up to mine. "But you'll be okay if you never taste blood. Stay away from their blood rituals, and you'll be fine."

Oh, boy.

Now this was officially worse than the "birds and bees" talk. At least with that one I could honestly say that I hadn't gone there yet.

But I'd tasted blood.

Not just tasted it either. I hungered for it. Just the thought of it now made my knees wobble and my heart pound. Even as my guts lurched at the thought of the hunt I'd just avoided, I still craved blood.

Mom didn't seem to notice my reaction.

"This is why the Initiation is so critical, you see. The temptation to drink blood drops exponentially when you're bound to the coven." Now her hands groped the air, drawing frantic pictures. "You see, the Initiation has the potential to destroy the desire entirely. It has something to do with the burden being shared by the group. But that's why I don't want you anywhere near vampires until you get another chance at it. I know you can pass if you get another chance. There was that puff of wind when all the candles blew out just as you called east. Are you sure that wasn't you, honey?"

I shook my head distractedly.

I should tell her about Thompson, shouldn't I? I mean, I had kind of mentioned it on the phone at the bowling alley, but she must not have gotten what I meant. She probably thought I was kidding around. Or maybe she didn't hear me.

"It was a strong coincidence, then. Are you absolutely positive? Maybe you can't feel your own magic working."

"What would happen to me if I tasted blood?"

"You don't want to know. Besides, the important thing is that you aren't going to, are you?"

"Uh. Maybe you should tell me what happens if I do."

"Why?"

"Remember the accident at gym? There was blood."

"You said you weren't hurt." Mom looked confused, but her

face tightened as the truth dawned. "You . . . what happened exactly?"

"That part I don't really know, but all of a sudden I had my lips on Thompson's nose and I kind of . . . no, I *totally* licked him."

Mom's mouth hung open for a moment. Then she started sputtering, like an engine that couldn't catch. Finally, she stopped and took a deep breath to start over. I could feel her calming herself, magical roots tapping the earth for steadfast strength. Finally, she said, "It might still be okay. There are rules for first blood. It has to be won in combat or taken from a sworn enemy."

"Check and check," I said. "Plus, Elias said it woke him up. It woke everybody up. Ramses is out there planning for my debut right now."

Mom's anger was explosive. There was a tiny bit of magic in it, and I felt the force of her power shove my chair back an inch or two.

"I will not allow it!"

It might have been my imagination, but I swear tiny lightning bolts crackled along the curls of Mom's hair. The power welling up in her, however, was hard to ignore. The whole house shook.

I stood up and held up my hands, as though in surrender. "Hey, it's going to be okay, Mom. Really." I just kept repeating that everything was going to be okay, because that was supposed to help calm people down, wasn't it?

The edges of Mom's clothes began to flap. A strong wind twisted around her. I felt it pull and tug at my hair. There was heat too, as if the furnace had kicked into double time.

I found myself scanning for the exit.

"No daughter of mine will be a bloodsucker," she announced.

She didn't seem to be talking to me anymore, but I replied anyway. "I'm really sorry about Thompson. Believe me. It was an accident."

The floor shifted beneath my feet. I fell into the wall. Books crashed from the shelves onto the rug.

Mom was having some kind of magical meltdown, and it was totally focused on me.

I had to get out.

"Hey!" I said, pointing out the window at the mulberry bushes. "Isn't that Dad?"

Mom's head swiveled like the scene in *The Exorcist* or that giant flaming eyeball in Mordor. For a brief moment, all her attention—and her power—shifted toward the window.

I dashed for the door.

I never made it. Magic slapped me hard in the back and I fell. Down, down, down into a spiraling darkness and oblivion.

Nineteen

The alarm woke me at seven. I blinked the sleep from my eyes and sat up slowly. Mom had tucked Berry Bear next to my pillow. I stared at his golden glass eyes and frowned.

It took me twenty minutes to decide what to wear. Every time I picked something out, a part of my brain would reject it as too trashy. When did all my clothes start to look so revealing? In the end, I put on a simple black turtleneck and my sparkly spider-web jeans.

Mom was making pancakes when I got downstairs. She was singing the circle song, and my frown deepened. A dream image skittered through my brain of dark woodland creatures and fangs.

"You look nice," Mom said, heaping a pile of pancakes onto a plate in front of my usual spot at the dining room table.

My stomach soured. I couldn't bring myself to sit down for some reason. I just wanted to get out and get going. "Uh, I'll grab something at the coffee shop," I said. "I don't want to be late."

She chewed her lip. Her eyes followed me anxiously to the door. "Well," she said. "Have a nice day."

It felt good to put my backpack over my shoulder and hear the door shut behind me. The air was chilly with the promise of autumn. The scent of fallen leaves woke up my sleeping senses.

Something was wrong.

I shook my head and stepped out into the yard. The juniper looked ragged and a pile of brownish needles lay scattered on the grass. I should rake, I thought.

Out past the gate and down the street. The neighborhood was going through its morning stretches. School buses rattled and screeched down the cobblestone streets. People carrying travel mugs of coffee stumbled to their cars, giving me a brief notice or a little wave. I smiled and hummed a little as I made my way to the coffee shop.

The lights were dim and the interior of the coffeehouse was moist and warm. As the door closed behind me, I was reminded of stepping into a dank underground cave.

I stopped as if slapped.

Suddenly, I was aware of Mom's spell covering me like layers of cobwebs.

I had no magic of my own to counteract Mom's snare, so all I could do was notice how perfectly it held me. The line of people inched closer to the cashier. I took the opportunity to study the spell. It was well crafted and heavy, like I was shrouded in a silvery fishing net. This was the sort of thing that took time and skill. She must have woven it after knocking me out.

The effect of the spell was that I felt sluggish and subdued. At least, I assumed that was part of the spell, and not a lack of my first dose of mocha. I had a sense that resistance was futile. Like

I had a bout of depression, I just wanted to lie down and let the world pass me by. Barring that, I'd go through the motions like a robot.

This was probably the spookiest, most evil and insidious spell I'd ever encountered. I'd be incensed and horrified that Mom cast it on me, only I couldn't quite work up the energy.

I had to do something!

Yawning, I shuffled another step or two closer.

In a haze, I ordered my coffee. I paid. I tipped. I sipped my mocha slowly and walked the rest of the way to my school bus stop. Skater-trash nodded. I nodded back.

This was awful. I felt like a prisoner in my own life. Hey, I wanted to shout to the skater boy, look at me! I'm trapped in here! Get me out!

But we just stood there, not talking, until the bus came and took us to school.

The janitor had removed the graffiti from my locker, at least. Taylor stopped by as I was organizing my books for the day. Organizing? Gah! Make it stop!

She watched my progress with raised eyebrows. "Someone needs more coffee," she teased. Today she had on a canary yellow *hijab* and matching Converses. A long-sleeved white turtleneck was tucked into slim jeans. Over the top, she'd put on a T-shirt with a picture of the bobble-headed Tweety Bird.

"Nice," I said, pointing. I mustered a smile.

Cocking her head at me, she said, "It's like you're an overseas call. Two-second delay."

"Tell me about it," I said, cradling my precalc text and notebook in my arms.

"You never answered my texts." She pouted. "What happened with Thompson, anyway? Rumor mill is abuzz. You kissed him. You licked his face. You smashed him with a runaway puck. He hates you. You love him. What's the real deal?"

I managed a laugh. "It's complicated."

She nodded like she believed it. We made our way down the crowded hall toward my classroom. "You missed drama. Did you skip? Were you sick?"

"I was so embarrassed by what happened in gym that I ran out."

Taylor gave me a sly look, then clapped her hands excitedly. "You did kiss him!"

It was what I told all my not-close friends, but I felt weird lying to Taylor. "No. You wouldn't understand. I'm being pulled between two worlds."

She arched her eyebrow. "You're kidding me, right? I am two worlds in one."

I raised my eyebrows in confusion.

She pointed to her *hijab*, and then to the cartoon bird. "I speak one language here and another at home. In more ways than one, you know?"

I was starting to. My brain felt stiff and my mouth slow and stupid, but I managed to say, "How do you choose?"

Taylor smiled. "Who says you have to?"

Huh.

I spotted Bea at the far end of the hall. Before I could stop myself, I'd waved. She waved back, but didn't make a move to come over. Then she did a classic double take. Bea probably sensed the spell hanging on me. I was pleased to notice her chewing her bottom lip for a moment before going back to shunning me.

"I wish you two would make up," Taylor said. "Why didn't you reply to her text? I know she's feeling hurt."

Hurt? I thought she was dissing me! My brain would have been jumping except it couldn't.

"Bea was supposed to throw you a belated birthday party this weekend. I already got permission from my dad to go. Now I don't think it's going to happen."

I didn't know what to say. "Bea wants to be friends?"

"Yes! Didn't I say that five minutes ago? Wake up! Everyone's been trying to talk to you. I sent you seven million messages last night. Where were you?"

"I went out with Nik," I said. We'd reached my class. Taylor had creative writing two doors down, so we lingered just outside. "Bowling."

"Oh my God, that's so cool!"

I smiled to imagine bringing Taylor along to Bryant-Lake Bowl sometime. She'd look awesome in her *hijab* and slippery shoes.

"He invited me to the house party tonight."

"You mean the one everyone is going to be at?"

"I guess," I said, unsure. I wondered if the spell would let me go, or if I'd drift home tonight and fall deep asleep like Sleeping Beauty.

"Thompson is going to be there. I hear he's taking Yvonne."

I rolled my eyes. Of course. Good for them. "That'll be awkward."

"You think?" Taylor smiled. The bell was about to ring, so she hurried off. "I can't believe you kissed Thompson. Nik is so much cuter."

No kidding. I wished I was with him instead of heading into math at nine in the morning.

The only good side effect of Mom's dampening spell was that nothing fazed me. I should have been absolutely in a panic at the thought of going to gym next period, but it all just seemed so ho-hum.

The girls in the locker room snickered at me, but I didn't even react with a blush. It was like Mom had given me armor plating against gossips. Well, that made this whole experience slightly less evil, I guess.

We did not, no surprise, continue with floor hockey. As we stood around and waited for instructions, Thompson glared at me from under his head bandage and blackened eye. I should have trembled at the sight, but the spell made me loopy, so I just lifted my fingers in little wave. I expected my little "hello" to piss him off, but instead he blushed and looked away.

His reaction made me wonder what kind of ribbing he'd had to face after I fled. Did *he* think I'd kissed him?

Wow, I should have been squirming. Instead, I just stood there like a perfectly poised mannequin.

Weird.

Mr. Johnson had us doing calisthenics—jumping jacks and the like. Somehow he filled an hour with drudgery and sweat. Ah, gym class.

Then, mercifully, it was over.

And somehow I managed to not embarrass myself, lick Thompson, or fall over in a stupor. I was starting to appreciate the subtler side effects of Mom's spell when Thompson bumped into me in the hall. I would have braced myself for a confrontation, but that would have been too much work. Instead, I let the wall prop me up as he loomed over me.

Yikes, he was menacing as all get-out. I stifled another yawn.

"What's wrong with you, witch?"

"Mom put a spell on me," I muttered.

Thompson frowned at my answer, but chose not to engage. "You have a strange way of telling people you like them. What is this, kindergarten? You going to throw a rock at me next?"

He totally thought I kissed him! "Dream on," I said.

He laughed. "You're the one who planted a wet one on me in front of the whole class. Pathetic!"

Having gotten in his parting shot, he stalked off. I watched him go. With a shrug, I propelled myself off the wall and back into motion, such as it was. Well, it could be worse. So he thought I was into him. I *did* think he was cute on those days he wasn't being a jerk, which was—let's see—never. But at least no one seemed to remember the truth—that I'd licked his cheek like an ice-cream cone.

I meandered unhurriedly to my locker to get books for American history. Ode to joy.

I stayed in a kind of pleasant haze until lunch, when I found myself staring at something that resembled a chicken patty. I was going through a routine of pick up sandwich, take a bite, replace sandwich on tray, chew, repeat, when someone sat down beside me.

I sighed, expecting Thompson and the whole "What are you doing by your lonesome?" routine again, but I was startled to discover Bea. She didn't look at me, but she began unwrapping the lunch she brought from home. She set out carrot sticks, a salami sandwich with mayo, and a cup of applesauce.

"Someone put a nasty spell on you," she said, talking to her sandwich. "Smells like your mom's work."

"Yep," I said through a mouthful of chicken pieces/parts.

"We haven't talked since the Initiation," Bea noted.

"Nope," I agreed, much, much less nervously than I felt. How did she feel about me? Were we still friends? Inside I was on pins and needles, but I could only blink slowly at her as if I were half asleep.

She shook her head at me, sadly, and sighed. "I was kind of shocked, you know, even though it wasn't entirely unexpected. It just . . ." She stopped and frowned darkly. She seemed to mull over something before she started up again. "Look, I don't know what to make of you in your new state, but we're friends. We've always been friends."

I could have kissed her, but I could only work up the energy to flop my hand on her arm and pat it mechanically. She patted me back.

"I'm so happy," I said, and went back to bite, chew, repeat.

"Well, I'm not. . . . That is, I'm not really there yet, you know, not ready to go back to the way things were, but I just can't abide this spell. It's not cool," she said, frowning at her carrot stick before taking a bite. "You might be half demon, but they shouldn't treat you like this."

"Like what?"

She spared a furtive glance at me. "Like one of their slaves."

If I could have expressed it, I would have been shocked. Bea must have gotten the whole vampire-witch history from someone if she knew that. But surely she'd been sworn to secrecy. Yet, here she was, talking to me. What was going on?

She started. "Where's my necklace?"

I pointed to my backpack.

"You should have kept it on. It might have helped protect

you. Bonds of friendship can be stronger than bonds of . . . oh, that's it. I think I know what we can do!"

Bea put a hand on my shoulder like she was giving me comfort, but I could feel her magic exploring the spell. "This is going to be complicated," she said, and I suspected she meant in more ways than the obvious. "Meet me before drama, and I'll have a fix."

"Really?" I'd meant to sound profoundly grateful, but it came out a touch bored.

Bea didn't seem offended. Instead, she nodded and chewed her carrot thoughtfully. "You might have to use your magic," she said. Our eyes met. "Yes," she said. "That's what I said. Your magic. See if you can dig some up before last period. Oh, and bring the necklace."

She didn't say anything more about it, and I was too bewildered to form any kind of coherent response or question. We ate the rest of the meal in silence, but just before it was time to clear our trays, Bea gave me a pat on the shoulder.

"It's going to be okay," she told me.

I gave her a zombie nod and shuffled off to class. Sluggish though my brain felt, it was also buoyed at the thought that Bea just might be my friend again. A slow, sleepy smile spread across my face.

As I WANDERED FROM CLASS to class, I tried to figure out what Bea meant by "your magic." Somehow I thought it must be more than my ability to sense when others did their thing, but what else did I have?

Had I done anything magical since the Initiation?

Well, I had developed fangs and a taste for blood. Oh, and I'd learned Zen and the art of seeing in the dark. Did she want me to do something vampiric?

I was still pondering this possibility when it was time to meet her at her locker. At first I thought she might have had a change of heart, because she was nowhere to be seen. Had she set me up just to be cruel?

Then I saw her rushing up. "Sorry," she said. "But I had to explain to Taylor why we might be a few minutes late for drama." Bea grabbed me by the arm and dragged me into the girls' bathroom.

The usual gaggle of girls was standing around the mirrors primping themselves before class. Bea dragged me into an empty stall. Locking the door, she whispered, "Bite me."

She rolled up the sleeve of her shirt and offered her wrist.

I stared at her. "Bite you?"

"Shhhh," she admonished, with a glance in the direction of the sinks. "Yeah, give it a good chomp." She waved her arm under my nose. "It's going to help, I think. You know, a blood bond. Your magic comes from blood, remember? Oh, and put on the necklace. Trust me."

As I dug the necklace out and slipped it over my neck, I pointed to my teeth. "No fangs."

"Well, shit. We don't have a lot of time before the bell. I told you to work this up. What does it take for them to show up?"

"Mad," I said. "Like the Incredible Hulk."

"You're ugly. That outfit is lame. Who dressed you this morning, your mama?"

"What?"

"I'm trying to make you mad, okay?"

I shook my head. This wasn't working. I pointed to my head. "Spell too heavy."

She stared at me. "Well, this sucks," she said, then gave me a guilty look. "No offense. But, you know, I'm kind of making this up. All right, I'll do part two now, and we'll try the biting after class." Bea closed her eyes for a second, and even through the thick fog of Mom's spell, I could feel her power rise. Bea's magic was always hot and quick, like lava or a spark. When her whole body was infused with the heat of it, she raised a finger. "Zap," she said as she touched the tip of the necklace.

It was if my neck were engulfed in flames. A searing pain lanced along the threads of the webbing of the spell. I cried out. The heat was intense. I felt like I was burning. Frantically, I tried to brush away the sensation.

Bea backed away, horrified. "Are you okay? Crap, I knew you needed blood first."

I couldn't form any words. The pain was too intense.

The bell rang.

"Okay, okay, don't panic," Bea said. She started digging through her purse for something. I tried to tell her I didn't think an aspirin was going to cover it, but then she pulled out a nail file and plunged the sharp end into her palm. It bounced off her skin. With a strangled curse, she tried again.

"It's time for your magic, girl," she said.

Clutching myself, I was nearly doubled over in agony when I sensed the presence of blood. It wasn't much. She'd managed only to scratch herself. Bea pressed the wound into my face. I lapped at it desperately.

A power started to rise in me. Where Bea's was bright and fiery, mine revved up more slowly, icily.

It began to build. Something deep inside me began to move. My stomach flip-flopped in rhythm to the growing energy. Faster and faster my world began to spin. Faster and faster, as the cold was replaced with a sizzling spark. I grabbed hard on to Bea's hand, as my whole world began to rotate. The lights flickered.

A slide and a click in my jaw, and down came my fangs. The moment my fangs emerged, I felt an electric pulse race along my skin. It blasted through the cottony web of Mom's spell like it was nothing.

My ears popped, and suddenly I could move; I was free. I could bite Bea now. I could use my sharp teeth and rip and tear her skin until blood flowed like wine. A snarl escaped my throat.

Bea sensed the change in me and tried to pull her hand from where I grasped it to my mouth. My grip tightened, and I shot her a possessive look.

"Class started," she reminded me, and I could feel a defensive spell boiling up under her skin, poisoning the sweet taste of the blood.

What was I doing?

I dropped her hand guiltily and straightened up, horrified at myself. I couldn't even contain my desire for blood when it was my sometime BFF; the hunt would have been a total disaster. My stomach started to roil at the thought.

"Oh, Bea. I'm so sorry!" I could tell by the tremble in my voice that her spell had worked. I was no longer under the cloud of Mom's spell. I started to dance with happiness. "It worked!" I hugged her tightly. "Oh, thank you! It worked!"

"We're going to be in so much trouble," Bea muttered. "You're kind of strong in your vampire form, by the way."

I laughed. I would have kissed her if I didn't think it would smear her cheek with blood. "Come on. We're only a few minutes late."

I started to pull her out the door, but she stopped me. "You need a napkin," she said, pointing to her own lips. In the mirror I could see what she meant. I looked like I'd had a very bad accident with a lipstick tube. She dug through her purse and offered me a Kleenex and found a Band-Aid for herself. "Okay," she said, snapping her purse shut. "Now we can go."

Mr. Martinez was none too pleased by our unexcused interruption. I pointed to Bea's palm and said we'd had to stop at the nurse's office. He seemed skeptical, and suggested that next time we should ask for a tardy slip. We nodded contritely and slipped into our seats.

While we continued reading the play, I noticed Bea watching me. Were my fangs still visible? I hadn't felt them slide back into wherever it was they came from, but no one was pointing and staring either.

I wished I could talk to her. She'd been so brave. I couldn't imagine it had been easy for her to decide to help me, especially when it meant giving me her blood. I wondered what made her change her mind. It must have really bothered her to see me caught in Mom's spell.

Speaking of which, I felt as though I just woke up. Everything was brighter, crisper. I could have broken out into song or danced a jig, but Mr. Martinez would have sent me to detention for sure. As it was, I was just grateful I'd been paying attention when it was my turn to read.

There would be a test on Monday, and everyone groaned

when Mr. Martinez reminded us to review the play and all our notes. We could expect essay questions.

Yet I couldn't keep a smile off my face. I would have floated out of the room, but Mr. Martinez called me back. Bea gave me a look that I hoped meant she'd wait for me. I nodded.

"I'm worried about you," he told me. "Your behavior has been very erratic. Are you using?"

Using? It took me a second to grasp his meaning. "Drugs? No. No way!" He looked at me as though he expected some sort of explanation. "There's some . . . trouble at home."

That was an understatement, but it seemed to satisfy him. "You know you can always talk to me. The school has counselors too."

Like I could tell them about my new interest in sucking people's blood!

"Yeah, thanks," I said, anxious to go.

"Go on," he said with a smile. "But do take care of yourself. I don't want to lose a good actress. There are so precious few."

A compliment from Herr Director? Would wonders never cease?

BEA AND TAYLOR WERE WAITING for me by Bea's locker. Taylor glanced between Bea and me curiously. "So we're all friends again?"

I started to nod enthusiastically, but Bea said, "We have a temporary truce."

Temporary?

"Does this mean the party is on?" Taylor asked.

"Party?" Bea asked.

Taylor's face fell. "Birthday. For Ana?"

"Oh," Bea said, looking at me. "Well, there is that house party at Nik's tonight. Should we make it a twofer?"

"I can't get into that," Taylor said. "It's sold out."

"You can get us in, can't you, Ana?" Bea said. There was an icy edge to her voice as she added, "Nik is your boyfriend, after all. What do you say?"

I got the impression that if I had any hope of making our truce permanent, I had no other option than to smile and say, "Sure!"

With Taylor hanging on excitedly chattering about the possibility of getting into THE social event of the season, I never got a chance to ask Bea what had motivated her to help me out. Especially since it was clear she was jealous of me and Nikolai.

And I had another, more serious problem. Mom would be able to tell we'd broken her spell. I could hardly waltz in like nothing had happened. I'd risk being snared up again.

But where to go? I considered calling Nik, but I knew he'd be busy getting ready for the big gig tonight. I didn't want to be in the way, especially since I needed to ask him a huge favor already. While I was thinking of it, I texted him to ask if it would be okay if I brought along two friends as guests. I buttered him up a bit by adding that from all accounts he was the hottest ticket in town. Maybe flattery would work. I had no idea how Bea would react if I couldn't come through with tickets.

I got onto the school bus and found a seat. I decided I might as well take it back to my neighborhood while considering where to go. The sun was hot on the vinyl seats. I was glad of the brisk

September breeze coming in from the half-opened windows. I squinted in the brightness.

Maybe I should try to find Elias. I felt like maybe I owed him an explanation for Nik and my quick escape last night. The thought of creeping through the underground of St. Paul, however, didn't appeal.

The bus bounced along. I watched traffic out the window. Soon we were turning down quieter streets, and I started to gather things together because I spotted my stop coming up.

And Mom waiting at the corner.

What was she doing there?

Twenty

Holy crap! Mom was waiting for me.

I slid down in my seat to avoid being noticed. Mom must have sensed the moment Bea and I shattered her spell. The bus came to the stop just before mine. I quickly grabbed my stuff and piled off with the group of girls. The bus driver gave me an odd look, but didn't say anything.

Meanwhile, I tried to blend. Luckily, this was a busy stop. There were a few little kids who had parents waiting for them, and I followed one of them, trying to act like we were all one big happy family. As soon as we turned the corner, I started to run.

The high I'd gotten from Bea's blood had worn off, and I found myself sweating in less than a block. The sun's heat seemed to drag my heels, but I kept going. I ran up the hill toward the University Club and then down the steep drop toward the children's hospital and the edges of downtown.

I had to slow down or risk tumbling down the sharply angled walk. I didn't think Mom had seen me get off early, but I checked behind me regularly. My phone rang, startling me. I dug it out. Mom, of course. No way I was answering that; I let it ring through to voice mail.

But it got me thinking. Could I call Bea? Maybe she'd let me hang out at her place until the party. No, her mom and mine were pretty tight. And besides, there was the temporary truce. I didn't want Bea to have to choose between witch and vampire again, especially since she'd seen me all bloodlusty and vamped out.

Taylor? I'd never been invited to her house. Of course, she'd never been to my house either. I wasn't allowed to bring home anyone who wasn't clued in to the True Witch thing.

It was times like this I wished I had more friends.

I'd made it to the bottom of the hill. Now where? I thought I might just try to find a coffee shop to hang out in. Rush hour traffic was beginning to rev up. Vehicles of all shapes and sizes crowded the narrow downtown streets. St. Paul didn't have much hustle, but knots of hospital workers in their Snoopy-decorated scrubs waited for city buses or walked briskly to parking ramps. Pinking sunlight glinted off glass windows. The industrial-cafeteria smell of the nearby café mingled with the scent of exhaust and city.

I settled into an easy pace. The city moved around me as the sun sank into the west. A five-foot-tall Woodstock statue painted dark blue to resemble deep space and decorated with white star clusters grinned at me as I passed. Up ahead, I spotted a café/coffee place.

The shop was crowded with after-work business, but I found a seat. I checked the time on my phone. The house party at Nik's wasn't until eight tonight. So, after buying an orange juice, I pulled out my homework and tried to concentrate on Shakespeare, the Great Depression, and calculus.

I was deep into a formula when my phone blipped. I glanced at it. A text from Nikolai! He said that my friends were always welcome to come to the gig, but he couldn't pick me up. Could I find a ride?

I was sure I could. If nothing else, there was the bus. I told him so. And then I reminded him to "break a leg."

He sent me back a smiley face two seconds later.

The coffee shop had emptied out as the sun faded. A glance toward the street showed the sidewalks were similarly quiet. I had to laugh. St. Paul had a reputation for rolling up its streets after five. It really seemed to be true.

You could tell that autumn was fast approaching. The sun was going down earlier and earlier. Soon, many office workers would be going to work in the dark and coming home as the sun set. They'd miss what little sunlight winter had to offer in Minnesota.

Bending my head over my books, I went back to studying. At this rate I was going to get an A average. But what else was there to do? I still had hours to kill before even considering heading over to Nikolai's.

I took a sip of OJ and sighed. What was I going to do? At least Bea was my friend again. Sort of. Anyway, I was just so grateful she helped me shake off the zombie spell. Where had my power come from? Vampires weren't supposed to have any magic beyond their superpowers.

Yet, if I concentrated, I could still feel tremors of an electric force, slipping back and forth, just under my skin. Absently, my fingers flipped through my science text, as if seeking the answer there. My gaze strayed to a picture of a magnet. There was some kind of diagram about building an electric current using a magnetic wheel, called a dynamo or something—I wasn't sure—but the image stopped me cold.

Hmmm, the energy was created by attraction and repulsion of two opposing forces. Magnets had two poles, a north and south, positive and negative. . . . A little like me. Hmmm, now, here was an interesting theory.

Maybe Taylor was right. Maybe not choosing one heritage or the other allowed me to access both, and the two conflicting polarities created the spark of energy between them—magic.

That made a lot of sense. I smiled at the thought. Cool. I finally had a power all my own.

But why had it originally felt cold, like ice?

Through the window, I watched a city bus lumber awkwardly around the corner. It was one of those superlong ones with the accordion division between the two halves.

I looked back at my science book, and scratched my head thoughtfully. Maybe my magic needed a jump start, like the dynamo had to have something to crank its wheel. Perhaps it felt cold because to get my energy moving, I'd had to draw energy from somewhere first. If I unconsciously pulled my own internal energy first, I might experience an actual drop in body temperature or something.

Which was why I'd had to taste Bea's blood! It was the thing that got my own magic rolling.

Okay, I was into this hypothesis. Now, if only I could test it in real life!

I smiled as I closed up my book. Being a science nerd paid off, after all. Now on to conquer American history—maybe I could find some clue about vampire culture buried in there. Ha!

THERE WEREN'T MANY ANSWERS IN American history, it turned out. When I looked up again, I felt someone watching me. I scanned the coffeehouse. It was virtually deserted. The barista busied himself behind the counter, and one other customer stared intently at something on her laptop screen. Otherwise, I had the shop to myself.

Outside, the darkness was complete, and I saw little besides my own spooked reflection, but I still felt the phantom sensation of eyes on my back.

Deciding it must be my imagination or maybe my constant watcher, Elias, I stood up and stretched my legs, which had started to cramp. The door opened to admit two men. They looked like a pair of Mormon missionaries, wearing white shirts, dark ties, dress pants, and trench coats. The only things they lacked were the bike helmets tucked under their arms. I started to turn back to my books, but they were walking intently in my direction in a way that made me reassess them.

The electric light glinted off their eyes, like cats'.

Vampires?

If they were, these two did not seem friendly.

I scooped up my books as fast as I could and craned my neck to locate an exit that would let me leave without going past them. But they were already to my table by the time I got my bag zipped and over my shoulder. One of them took my elbow in a vise grip.

"Time to go," he told me. Then his lip curled as he added, "Princess."

I tried to pull out of his grasp. "Let me go."

He hissed, showing me his fangs. His friend shook his head. "Quickly," the other said, glancing behind himself as though checking for something. "The guard will be here any minute."

Did he mean Elias?

The other guy wrenched me toward the door. I kicked him in the shins, but to no avail. "Help!" But there was no sign of the computer woman or the barista. I shouted again, louder.

"No use," the other said, coming up to take me by my other elbow. "We own St. Paul at night."

Despite my fear, I almost laughed. No wonder St. Paul had a legendary reputation for rolling up its streets at night! People always made excuses about us being very Norwegian or very insular, but now it made a kind of sense. People were hiding from vampires.

I wished there were someone to see me now, when I needed help. Of course, there was no one. Maybe vampires exuded some kind of cloaking spell to keep the few people who might be out from noticing us.

Not knowing what else to do, I went limp, making them drag me out the door. They snarled and spat, but their strength was surprising and they managed to get me out into the street. Even though there was no one in sight, I kept yelling for help. Maybe if Elias was close by, he would hear me.

As panic raced along my veins, I felt coldness move slowly outward from my solar plexus. My heart rate slowed, calming me. A sharp pain in my gums signaled that my fangs had dropped. My limbs felt heavier, and I sensed my captors struggle more to propel me along. The night became less dark, and I was able to kick at their ankles with more precision and force. My vampire powers, apparently, were coming out to play.

They exchanged a worried glance, but tightened their grip.

A semitruck rattled down a distant street, but otherwise it was quiet enough that I could hear the click of the signal light as it switched to "walk." Parked cars crowded along the curbs, hood to trunk, but their occupants were nowhere in sight.

"Where are you taking me?" I demanded, trying to sound authoritative.

"To your mother, the queen."

Twenty-one

y mother, the what?

They couldn't really mean *my* mother, could they?

"You're vampires, right?" I asked them, as I continued to try to delay our progress down the street. Their lips curled, so I corrected, "Knights of the dark realm, I mean."

One of them spat. The other said, "We are knights in the service of the queen."

Right, these guys were the ones who wanted to be slaves, slaves to the . . . oh my God, to the witches!

Was Mom queen of the witches?

She'd talked on and on about legitimacy and treaties. . . . You didn't make treaties with just anyone, did you?

"My mother is the queen of witches?"

They looked at me like I had just asked if the night was black. I could almost read the "Duh" behind their eyes. "Of course."

"But—but," I sputtered, "there's not supposed to be hierarchy. . . . It's—it's . . ." All just a cover for outsiders, I realized. By the way she bitched about them, the Elder Witches obviously had some power over my mom, but she had a lot of power in the coven. That's why Mom insisted I had to pass the Initiation before she could explain about Ramses. That's why Mom was so confident I'd pass, and why she kept insisting I get another chance.

"Holy crap," I muttered.

They dragged me through a small park the size of a city block. A man-made river gurgled over brass-sculptured waterfalls. Birch trees dropped yellowing heart-shaped leaves on pavement and among the tufts of ornamental grass. We passed under a miniature band shell, and my shouts of protest reverberated enough to scare a squirrel up into a tree and launch a troop of pigeons into flight.

The vampire thugs brought me to the entrance of an office building. It was an older building with a stone facade. Decorative carvings ran along the edges of the windows and the rooftop. Only a few lights shone through small panes.

In order to get me inside, they had to open the door. One of them released his hold on me, which gave me an opportunity to wriggle from their grasp. I wedged my tennis shoes into the edges of the door. Splaying my arms out, I grabbed the frame and held tight. Now that I knew that it was Mom they were taking me to, I fought even harder. No way in hell was I going in there. She'd put another zombie spell on me, at the very least.

At that moment, the cavalry arrived, though it seemed more like a Mafia hit in retrospect.

From somewhere behind me, I heard the squeal of brakes. Car doors opened and slammed shut. Suddenly, the pressure behind me was gone. The guy yanking on my arms looked up in horror and fled. Panting from the exertion of my resistance, I spun around, ready to face whatever new threat had appeared.

Elias held a huge, silvery gun pointed at the chest of my former assailant. Two other men I didn't recognize held him firmly. I was about to ask Elias what was going on when he made the sign of the cross over the Mormon-looking guy and pulled the trigger.

I cringed, expecting a loud explosion. But the gun must have had a silencer. There was a soft noise, and the guy's body jerked where the bullet ripped through his chest.

A tiny gasp escaped my throat. I expected the guy to crumble to dust or do a vanish-except-for-his-clothes Obi-Wan Kenobi. Instead, he slumped limply. His eyes stretched wide in horror and shock, unblinking.

He was dead.

Had I been wrong about him? Had he been human after all? My stomach convulsed. The one weird thing was that there was no blood that I could see. You'd think with a gunshot wound at such close range, there'd be spatters everywhere. Did vampires bleed? Maybe he was a vampire, after all?

All I knew was that I felt sick. The longer I stared at the body, the more my stomach gurgled unhappily.

Elias slid his gun into a holster under his coat and made a motion to the two holding the body. They dragged him to the car and, quite unceremoniously, dumped him in the trunk.

Too horrified to really react, I let Elias gently lead me to the car. "We must go, my lady."

"That guy is dead," I said. My eyes stayed riveted to the trunk as Elias opened the car door for me. "You killed him. Shot him."

Elias nodded patiently and helped me into the passenger-side seat. I went with no resistance. "It is regrettable," he said. "I do not relish dispatching our own, but he chose his fate."

"So he was a vampire . . . or demon," I said, feeling strangely relieved. "You can just shoot demons?"

"If you have a special gun," he said.

"Silver bullets?"

"Magic." He closed my door. In the rearview mirror, I watched the two other vampires slide into the backseat, and had my first good look at them. One of them was an Asian man with long, flowing hair tied back into a ponytail. The very front of his forehead, where his bangs would be, was shaved. The other vampire was a black man with short-cropped hair. He gave me a wink and a smile when he noticed me watching them both. I returned the smile, though my mind was stuck on the image of a dead man being shoved into the trunk of this very car. I shivered at the thought of being so close to an actual corpse.

The door opened and Elias dropped easily into the driver's seat. He turned and spoke to the two in the back in Greek. Okay, it could have been Japanese or German, but suffice it to say it wasn't English and I had no idea what he said. They did, apparently, because they nodded as though in understanding.

"Where's the other guy?" I asked. I thought I'd spotted three others before.

"Gal," Elias corrected lightly as he started the engine. "The lieutenant has gone after your other attacker. With luck, she will stop him before he alerts the queen."

"Who is my mom—did you know?"

Elias opened his mouth with a look of surprise, but then a commotion from inside the building distracted his attention. I followed his gaze. A group of people could be seen running out the door I'd struggled so hard not to go through. Elias hit the gas. We sped away before they even hit the sidewalk.

"It appears the lieutenant failed," Elias remarked drily.

The way the lights were timed in downtown, Elias made it only up the block before hitting a red. He hesitated only a second before shooting through the intersection. Even though there was no obvious cross-traffic, I squeezed my eyes shut until we made it across. Then I double-checked my seat belt.

I heard clicks from the back.

When I glanced in the rearview, the Asian guy gave me a better-safe-than-sorry shrug.

"What just happened?"

"I ran a red."

"No, I meant back there."

"You were nearly abducted, my lady," Elias said.

"I know that, but why?"

"That part I don't know."

Suddenly, someone appeared in the middle of the street in front of us. Instinctively, Elias hit the brakes. I should've known it was a trap. No one is out on the streets of St. Paul after dark. Too late, we discovered the ambush. The moment he stopped, we were surrounded by vampires.

"Time to surrender, Captain." It was Mom's voice.

Twenty-two

Elias revved the engine menacingly. I put my hand on the steering wheel. "That's my mom! Don't even think about it."

"How about I just back over the ones behind us?"

"Or the ones on the sidewalk," one of the guys in the backseat suggested.

"Be serious," I said, though I thought they might have been. I unbuckled my belt. "I'm going out there."

Elias touched my knee imploringly. "This is a mistake," he said. "But if you face them, we will stand beside you."

The two guys in the back nodded. From somewhere, the Asian guy produced an elegant katana and the other a curved scimitar.

What was this, a video game? And anyway, who brings a sword to a gunfight?

The threat, however, was obvious.

"I don't want a fight. It's not going to come to violence," I said. "Maybe I can talk to Mom, get her to understand."

"That we should be free?" Elias raised an eyebrow. "Perhaps you are a better negotiator than all the emissaries of the dark realm."

"She's my mom," I said, reaching for the latch. "I think I've got a bit of pull."

I hoped I did, because there were a whole lot of them and only four of us. I swallowed and closed the door behind me. The sound bounced hollowly through the tall buildings.

Mom stepped forward. It would have made a better scene if she'd changed into something billowy and queenly, but she still wore her academic drag: a knee-length skirt, sensible shoes, a blouse, and a shapeless coat. Her glasses glinted under the street-lights, obscuring her eyes.

I walked around to the front of the car to meet her. Elias instantly appeared at my side. The other two, literally, watched my back.

A grim smile spread across Mom's face. "I see you brought me the Praetorian Guard. A nice coup."

"This is no surrender," Elias said. "We parley."

Snickers drifted through the collection of vampires, but Mom raised her hand to stifle them. "Parley accepted," she said.

"What's a parley?" I whispered to Elias.

"Think of it as a negotiation on the field of battle," he said. I noticed he'd taken his gun out of its holster at some point. He held it loosely at his side. It was some sort of semiautomatic. I had no idea how many bullets were in a gun like that, but even if he was a crack shot, I doubted he could take out all the loyalist vampires before they got us.

Plus, I recognized a few faces in the crowd. Desperately, I tried to see Nikolai or his dad—would I even recognize his father? Did I look for a guy in Gypsy gear with a psychic knife?

Or were they hiding in the shadows?

Mom had brought along some coveners, including Bea's dad. This could be really bad. Elias and his crew were outgunned in more ways than one.

We were totally screwed.

We had stopped near a covered parking lot that doubled as the farmers' market. Pseudo-old-fashioned streetlamps held glowing orbs. Industrious spiders had stretched their webs between every available surface. The air had grown chilled and smelled of river. I straightened my jacket.

"Just one question," I said, trying, mostly successfully, to keep my voice from quaking. "What do you want from me, Mom?"

Mom's posture shifted. She drew herself out, as though softening a little. "It's not like that. I don't want anything from you, honey. I just want to protect you from these"—I could hear the sneer in her tone—"*rebels* until you have a chance to take the Initiation test again."

Probably, I should have been offended. She sneered at my friends and, clearly, had ordered a couple of guys to abduct me, but I sort of understood her position. She sounded like a mom. She didn't want me getting hurt or mixing with the wrong crowd, as it were.

If that was all, that would be the end of it. We could apologize, hug, and go home to a nice cup of hot chocolate.

There was just one really huge problem. "What about first blood? I'm a vampire now, Mom. It's too late to protect me."

"No, listen, I've discovered a way around that. We can bind you."

Elias stiffened. The two vampires behind me likewise shifted uncomfortably and raised their swords slightly.

"Binding?" I whispered to Elias.

"Enslavement," he said.

"Don't get advice from that creature," Mom said. "It wouldn't be like that, I promise."

Somehow I doubted it. Even without Elias's clarification, binding didn't sound like a good thing.

At my hesitation, Mom added, "I've consulted all the Elders. This could work. We would bind your vampire side to your witch side. Your will would still be your own. You'd serve yourself."

It was a neat little solution, if a little fuzzy on the details.

A shout came from the rooftop. "Laudable, Amelia, but you neglect something vitally important." It was Ramses. We craned our necks to locate him. I finally spotted him behind Mom, crouching on the ledge surrounding the flat roof of the parking lot. He peered down at us over the ENTER ONLY sign. His elbows rested casually on the *L*.

"The binding talisman is well lost. You can't use it against us anymore," Ramses said. "To do what you suggest, you'd have to destroy the vampire in our daughter. How are you going to do that?"

Mom apparently didn't have a good answer, because she shouted, "Seize them!"

Then all hell broke loose.

Ramses had not come alone. The instant that the people surrounding us surged forward, vampires started dropping out of the sky from every rooftop.

Elias didn't hesitate for a second. His gun rose to the ready, and he gently shoved me behind him. At the same time, with military precision, his men closed ranks.

Ramses' army nearly matched Mom's to a person. I noticed that a group of vampires guarded Mom the same way Elias's men did me. Mom shouted for someone to "protect the witches," at the same time Ramses commanded his people to "grab the witches."

I tried to spot Bea's dad. Desperately, I tried to see my other friends from the coven. From what I could tell over the shoulders of my protectors, it was all chaos. I wished they wore uniforms. I couldn't tell which ones were Mom's guys and which belonged to Ramses. Most of the people were unarmed and fighting with fist, claw, and tooth. A few seemed to be carrying clubs or chains.

No one had weapons but Elias and his two men. Elias could have used his gun offensively, picking off Mom's guys one by one, but he didn't. Instead, he made no aggressive move.

This was crazy. There was an all-out vampire rumble in the middle of downtown. Where were the cops!?

I swung my backpack around and started digging through it for my phone. Elias seemed to sense my movement, though he never took his eyes away from the fight surrounding us. "What are you doing, my lady?"

"Dialing 911," I said.

Elias nodded as though he approved. "A cunning strategy in its own way. I wonder if it will work."

I didn't have time to ask him what he meant by that. I found the cell. Quickly, I punched the numbers, even though my fingers shook so hard I thought for sure I'd misdial. I could barely hear the operator when we connected. She asked me something about the state of my emergency.

"There's a huge fight in downtown St. Paul near the farmers' market," I told her. Then, because I thought I might get a quicker response, I added, "There's a ton of them. I think it might be gang related. And there's guns! And drugs! And I have to go!"

She wanted details, like my name and address, but I hung up. I hoped the police hurried. At least both sides seemed to be at a stalemate.

That's when I felt the low-level hum of magic vibrating below my feet. "Oh no," I said. "They're going to use magic!"

Elias shifted, and he trained his weapon on someone. Looking down the length of his arm, I saw he had his sights on Mom.

"No!" I shouted, grabbing at his shoulder, trying to pull down his arm.

"But if they coordinate their magic, it's over for us."

"You can't kill my mom!" I had to do something. Maybe I could tap my power somehow. I just needed that jump start.

"She wouldn't hesitate to do the same to me," he muttered.

I ignored his comment. "Let me bite you," I said suddenly, surprising myself almost as much as him.

For the first time since the fight began, he shifted all his attention to me. "What?"

"Bea taught me this trick. I think I can counteract their magic. Or at least make my own. Hurry," I said, feeling the cold surge begin. "Give me your arm!"

The black guy with the scimitar took a hit; his head whipped back and he fell almost right in front of Elias's feet. Someone must have thrown a rock at him. He was cradling his head and struggling slowly to his feet. Elias swore in that language I couldn't understand.

Elias tucked his gun into his holster, and pushed up the sleeves of his coat and shirt. Tucking his thumb under my chin for a moment, he caught my eyes. Very seriously he said, "Freely given."

The Asian guy noticed what we were doing, and he took in a sharp breath. "Captain?"

"You heard the words, Lieutenant," he said sharply. Then to me, he said, "Your pleasure, my lady."

"Okay," I said, since he seemed to want a response from me. My fangs were still out, so I grabbed his wrist and bit down hard. His blood exploded in my mouth.

Twenty-three

The sensation overwhelmed me. I thought I knew what to expect when I tasted blood, but Elias's was, if possible, even stronger, more intense. It rushed through me like an electric current. Every nerve ending danced as the world began to spin again. My body shook and convulsed as I tried to hold on to his wrist as I drank.

I would have let go, but it was working.

The rush of Elias's blood was a much bigger push than Bea's. Internally, I could feel my energies begin to flip between vampire and witch. My theory in practice! It was astounding how much the sensation did feel like a dynamo spinning. The spark of energy flashed like a strobe along my nerve endings. This time, it had no zombie webbing spell to burn through, so it continued to rise and rise. I needed to direct it.

I focused my will using the skills I'd so desperately tried to hone as a witch. I urged the ice to flow into the ground. I imagined it spreading outward in a circle like an ice-skating rink.

Beneath my feet the tremors of the coveners' magic stilled, stalled . . . froze.

In fact, time seemed to stop.

For a second, I stood outside of it all. I could see the whole event from the outside. Surrounded by her followers, Mom's face showed a slow realization that my magic had dampened the combined forces of five True Witches. Ramses, in the thick of hand-to-hand combat, sensed a change in the tide of the battle. Bea's dad and the other witches had been knocked off their feet by the blast and were frozen in midfall.

Cool.

I did that.

And I so wanted to snap a pic with my cell so I could send it to my friends.

When I let go of Elias's wrist, everything snapped back into motion—sort of. Slowly everyone dropped their fists and lowered their weapons. Their attention swung to the center of the circle to where I stood with Elias's blood on my lips.

No one moved. The street was silent.

In the distance, the sirens wailed.

Ramses took a measured step forward. Then, with a flourish, he dropped to one knee. The instant he did, all his people followed suit. Beside me, Elias did likewise.

Mom's mouth hung open. "That was you," she whispered. "Your magic."

I nodded, not trusting myself to say anything else. The sirens seemed right on top of us now.

"Behold your true heir," Bea's dad shouted. "She who walks between the worlds." Apparently, this was very meaningful because gasps and whispers rippled through the ranks of those who remained standing.

Pretty soon everyone was on their knees.

Except for Mom.

And me.

We faced each other in the middle of the street. Mom's face twitched, like she didn't know what to say or do.

So I ran over to her and gave her a great big hug.

For a second, she stood stiffly, not reciprocating. Then I heard a sniff, and her arms wrapped tightly around me.

There were cheers and joyful shouts.

When I pulled out of the embrace, Mom had tears in her eyes. She frowned into my face. With her thumb, she wiped at my lip. "You were always a messy eater."

Red and white lights reflected on the buildings. The police were nearly on us. "Scatter!" I heard her command her people. Ramses similarly told his people to run, but he stayed, coming to stand beside us.

"I was wrong," he said quietly. "Our daughter is stronger when she stands between our worlds. To try to make her a full vampire would have been a mistake."

I looked at Mom. Would she agree? I could see her face tighten. She didn't want to admit defeat. Finally, she said, "It's hard to deny what happened."

They looked at each other for a long time. Ramses was the first one to speak. "Cease-fire."

"Yes," Mom said curtly, her arms still wrapped tightly around my waist. "I will agree to that. But now you go away and don't come anywhere near my daughter."

I started to say something, but Elias came up to stand beside his prince. "That's impossible. Ana and I have joined in a blood bond. She is my betrothed."

"Like we're engaged?" I sputtered, breaking from Mom's grasp to stare at Elias. He was gorgeous and I liked being his lady and all, but I wasn't ready to be anyone's wife or even fiancée.

A police car moving at full speed up the street caused us all to run for the sidewalk. It didn't stop, but seemed to be in pursuit of someone else.

"Was it freely given?" Ramses asked Elias.

I remembered what he'd said. "But," I said. "But I didn't know!"

"You would reject the captain of the guard?" Ramses looked shocked.

"You bet she would," Mom said, looking ready to get up into everyone's faces.

"No, I accept," I said quickly, because I wanted Mom out of my business, and I figured there was probably some way out of it eventually.

Mom's face twisted angrily.

Ramses nodded his head. Looking between Elias and me, he smiled slightly. "Perhaps," he said, "we will someday have a true peace between our people."

My mom muttered something that sounded like "over my dead body," but she cleared her throat. "For now we'll be satisfied with a cease-fire. That crea— The captain may visit Ana only under the strict rules of courtship. Are we agreed?" Mom glared at Elias, daring him to make a fuss.

I had no idea what the rules of courtship were, but I was

happy I'd get to see Elias. "What do you say?" I asked him encouragingly. I could still taste his sweet blood on my tongue.

Elias looked at me and smiled. He bowed his head in that courtly way and touched his heart. "As you wish," he said.

My phone buzzed in my pocket. I'd forgotten I tucked it there after I'd called the police. I glanced at it. A message from Bea: "Where are you? The party's started."

"Uh," I said. "I've got to go."

～⁀ Twenty-four

I t took some fancy talking to explain everything to Mom, but when she heard that the party was at Nikolai's, she offered to drive me there herself. I guiltily left Elias with a quick peck on the cheek. I promised him we'd talk soon. He looked disappointed, but was, as usual, a perfect gentleman about it.

Mom and I were halfway there before she decided to talk. "There's a way to break the betrothal, you know," she said. "It's not hard, just formalized."

"I'm not interested right now," I said. Thing was, I knew that if I broke things off with Elias, Mom would find a way to keep me from seeing any vampires. I wasn't ready for that yet. At the very least, I figured I still had a lot to learn about being half vampire. Plus, I liked Elias. There was something about him, what with that catlike grace and all his courtly airs. I wasn't about to break his heart. Not yet.

"Are you and Nikolai dating?"

"Not officially," I said. And that was the other thing. I liked

Nikolai, but I wasn't entirely ready to be his full-time girlfriend. Not until I really understood how he felt about vampires. He could be so scary. But then again, he could be superhot.

I wondered whether Nikolai would be disappointed that he missed the big fight. Or maybe his dad had been there all along. . . . I had no idea. I'd think about that later.

Mom sniffed. "I think Nikolai might be kind of upset to discover you're engaged to marry the captain of the Praetorian Guard, don't you think?"

"He doesn't have to know, does he, Mom?"

"You're going to date them both?"

Was I? "I'll work it out," I told her. "My way."

Mom didn't say anything for a long time. Finally, she said, "All right."

What was this? Trust? From Mom?

She seemed to sense my surprise, so she said, "You proved yourself pretty capable tonight, honey. I'm just going to have to trust that I raised you right, and that you'll make smart decisions."

"Really?"

Mom sighed. "Just. . . ." She turned down Nikolai's street. Cars lined the block. I pointed to his apartment, and she put the car in park. "Just be home by midnight, Cinderella."

I gave her a hug and a quick kiss. "Thanks, Mom!"

JOHN WAS SITTING ON A stool just inside the downstairs door checking for tickets. He was arguing with a couple that I recognized as Thompson and Yvonne. "I'm sorry," John was saying as I came up. "You can't come in. You don't have tickets."

When he saw me, he waved around them. "Hey, Ana! About time, girl! Nik's been wondering where you've been."

The look Thompson gave me was pure envy. "You know the band?" he muttered as I flounced happily past him. It took every ounce of strength I had not to stick my tongue out at him and sing the "nyah, nyah, nyah" song.

"Excuse me," I said, bumping him slightly. Okay, so I had to be a little snotty!

Thompson muttered something about how the party must be full of freaks anyway as he dragged Yvonne off the steps with him. John and I watched them go. I couldn't quite stifle a smile. How satisfying was *that*?

"Your friends are already here," John said. "I thought you were a no-show for sure."

"I had a little family business to take care of."

John nodded like that made perfect sense. "Families," he muttered. "Can't live with 'em, can't live without 'em."

"You could say that," I said with a smile.

"You should head down. I know Nik will be happy to see you," he said.

"Down?"

He pointed to a door I hadn't noticed before on one side of the entry. "Basement rec room; it's totally why we rented this place."

I thanked him and bounded down the stairs. The door to the rec room was open, and I could see that the place was packed. Ugly seventies paneling covered the walls. Basement windows near the ceiling had been cracked open to let air into the stuffy room. Multicolored linoleum tiles lay across the floor. The space had a surprisingly high ceiling and someone had hung a disco ball in the center of the room. Dots of light spun slowly around the gyrating bodies.

I stood at the doorway trying to figure out how to even wedge myself in. In the thick of it, I could see Bea and Taylor dancing together near the makeshift stage at the far end. They looked absolutely ecstatic. And why shouldn't they? Just standing there, I felt my shoulders relax for the first time in days. A smile spread across my face. Despite what Thompson said, I wasn't a freak anymore. I knew who I was. I was a dhampyr, a princess of both the vampires and the witches, and a girl who was about to have the time of her life. . . .

Just watch me.

About the Author

Tate Hallaway lives in St. Paul, Minnesota. She is also the author of the Garnet Lacey novels. Visit her on the Web at www.tatehallaway.com or check out her blog at tatehallaway.blogspot.com.